‘I have a problem here,’ Charlie confessed.

‘I’m not sure who I am.’

‘You’re not sure?’ Tessa glared. This was getting crazier and crazier.

‘Well...’ Charlie’s blue eyes glinted with laughter. ‘Until a week ago, I was Charles Cameron, cattle farmer. But now...according to this, I’m Lord Charles Cameron, thirteenth Earl of Dalston. Owner of a grand-sounding title, and—if you’ll agree to marry me—owner of one rather decrepit castle and all it contains...’

Trisha David is a country girl, born on a south-east Australian dairy farm. She moved on—mostly because the cows just weren't interested in her stories! Married to a 'very special doctor', Trisha writes medical romances as Marion Lennox and Enchanted stories as Trisha David. In her other life she cares for kids, cats, dogs, chooks and goldfish, she travels, she fights her rampant garden (she's losing) and her house dust (she's lost!)—oh, and she teaches statistics and computing to undergraduates at her local university.

Recent titles by the same author:

BORROWED—ONE BRIDE
FALLING FOR JACK

BRIDE BY FRIDAY

BY
TRISHA DAVID

First published in Great Britain 1998
Harlequin Mills & Boon Limited,
Eton House, 18-24 Paradise Road, Richmond, Surrey TW9 1SR

ISBN 0 263 81228 6

Set in Times Roman 10½ on 11½ pt.
02-9811-50354 C1

Printed and bound in Norway
by AiT Trondheim AS, Trondheim

CHAPTER ONE

'MARRY me?'

'I...I beg your pardon?'

On second thoughts, maybe this *was* rushing things. He'd been sitting beside Tessa Flanagan for all of five minutes.

'It was just a thought,' Charlie said hastily. Uh-oh. His gorgeous fellow passenger was staring at him as if he'd landed from Mars, and he really had only been thinking aloud. How to retrieve a situation like this?

If ever there was a time to lay on the Cameron charm, this was it.

Charles Cameron lifted a pile of papers from his drop-down table, and let it fall again as if the weight of the pile explained all. Then he sighed, giving Tessa the benefit of his very nicest smile. It was a totally heart-stopping smile, and it usually worked a treat.

'I know it's sudden, but the way I'm reading this, it's either marriage or lawyers,' he told her. 'And you sure beat lawyers!' Charlie directed his fantastic smile straight at Tess, and it showed absolute appreciation.

Which just showed how deranged the man was, Tess decided, staring at him in astonishment. She hadn't slept since she'd heard about Christine. Tessa's trim figure was disguised by the jogging suit she was wearing for comfort on the long flight. Her short, blonde curls were tousled and unkempt, and her eyes were shadowed and way too large for her face.

And this man—a complete stranger—was asking if she'd marry him!

She eyed him warily for all of ten seconds, as if he was about to sprout Martian antennae. Charlie kept smiling. Finally Tess came to the conclusion that he was nuts, but harmless nuts. Maybe even nice nuts.

'Yeah, right,' she said blankly and turned away, trying to block him out.

She couldn't block out his presence. Nutcase or not, Charles Cameron was a difficult man to block.

Charlie was six foot three without his boots on. He had broad shoulders, but he didn't carry one ounce of spare fat. The man was sheer muscle, his body narrowing to long, long legs stretched out under the airline seat. He was wearing a short-sleeved, open-necked shirt and moleskin trousers, and his clothes suited his muscled, tanned and weather-beaten body to perfection.

Despite her distress, it was impossible for Tess to ignore the sheer maleness of the man. He was thirty or so and weathering magnificently. Charlie's thick black hair was bleached at the tips as if exposed to too much harsh sun. His deep blue eyes twinkled and danced and made you want to smile...

He looked a man apart. Charles Cameron fitted into the surrounding sea of suits like a bull fitted into a china shop— and Charles Cameron was some bull!

Oh, for heaven's sake... Ignore him, Tess thought desperately, as she clenched her eyes shut. She had enough to worry about without a grinning lunatic she'd never met before proposing marriage from the neighbouring seat.

Like thinking about Christine...

The thought of Christine was enough to stop any hint of a smile. Christine was Tessa's twin sister—and Christine was dead.

Maybe it was stupid for Tess to feel this bad. Donald

had told her over and over that she shouldn't care. He didn't understand Tessa's grief-stricken reaction one bit.

'For heaven's sake, Tess, you haven't seen Christine or your snobbish brother-in-law for six years. Not since your twenty-first birthday. She met that creep and she hasn't been home since. She's hardly written. They didn't even come to your mother's funeral. And you've never been to England to visit her. You've never even wanted to visit...'

That was how much Donald knew! Tess had ached to visit her twin, and she longed to travel.

But Tess couldn't ignore family ties as Christine had done. Their mother had been an invalid and, after her death, her legacy of medical bills had made visiting Christine impossible.

And now Christine was dead. Her mother was gone, and now her sister. It was the end of her family.

Only it wasn't the end, of course. There was Ben...

She *had* to see him. She must! Even if she wasn't wanted.

'Hey, if it's my proposal making you look like this, then forget it.' The deep male voice rumbled beside her and Tessa's eyes flew open. It was such a nice voice. Low and growly, but warm and with such depth...

The lunatic's voice. The Martian.

For a moment, Tess wished she was back in her economy class seat—but only for a moment. As a last-minute passenger, she'd been wedged between a twenty-stone woman who reeked of garlic, and the airline toilet. The tap on her shoulder after the hour's stop at Singapore—'Miss, we have a seat available in business class if you'd like the offer of a free upgrade'—had been a gift from heaven.

'Am I making you look like this?' the man asked anxiously, and then answered his own question. 'Nope. I'm sure it's not me. You looked like this before.'

'Like what?' Tess asked before she could help herself, and the man smiled his blindingly attractive smile.

'Like a mermaid who's lost her sea,' he said gently. 'Who's floundering on the beach and who doesn't know how to get home.'

A mermaid. Honestly!

Tess glared. 'I just need some sleep,' she managed.

'Hey, I guessed that,' he told her. 'That's why I suggested you come up here.'

'You suggested...'

'The seat beside me was empty all the way from Australia.' He grinned at her look of astonishment. 'I stretched out and luxuriated no end but, truth to tell, I was lonesome. Then I saw you in Singapore looking like a waif who was about to topple over, and I thought if there was company to be had I wouldn't mind if you were it. So I pointed you out to the airline people and told them you looked too young to be travelling alone.' His smile deepened. 'They agreed—and here you are.'

'They agreed...' The man's audacity took Tessa's breath away. So that was why she was sitting in business class.

She'd wondered. She looked unimportant and unkempt—the last person suitable for an upgrade to business class. But now... As well as having to humour an obvious lunatic, she also had to be grateful.

'Thank you,' she said stiffly. 'But—'

'But you have to sleep and I've just thrown you a proposal that's got you all in a tizz,' he said sagely. 'I can see that. Don't answer all at once. Tell you what. You catch forty winks while I sift through these papers again and see if there isn't any other way out of this mess—and we'll talk about it later.'

His smile was warm and gentle and infinitely comforting. As if he weren't a lunatic at all.

'Here,' he said, offering her an eye mask. 'And here.' A pillow and blanket were added to the ones the hostess had already given her. 'Now just push this little button...' He leaned over and pushed the little button and her seat sank back to almost fully reclining. Then, to her absolute bewilderment, he kissed her lightly on the nose. 'Sweet dreams. See you in London!'

And he placed her eye mask over her eyes and left her to her confusion.

Tessa slept the clock around, and when she opened her eyes her first thought was that she was warm and cared for and that the nightmare had receded.

She was being held.

She opened one eye cautiously—and then another.

In sleep, her head had drooped sideways. The man by her side was now wearing a cashmere jumper—soft and warm and bulky. His seat was also reclining. She was using the stranger's sweater— his shoulder!—as her pillow, and she could hear the beating of his heart under her right ear.

She sat up as if she'd been hit by an electric cattle prod, and the broad arm around her shoulders was reluctantly withdrawn.

'Hey,' the man said dolefully. 'I was asleep.'

'I'm so sorry.' Tessa struggled sideways in a muddle of blankets and tried to make her eyes work. The cabin lights were dim and the darkness was intimate.

Sleeping with a stranger...

'No need to be sorry.' The arm came back around, possessive and strong. 'Half an hour till they turn on the lights for breakfast. Snooze a little.'

'What...what time is it?' Still she struggled, hauling herself back in the luxurious comfort of her velvet seat.

He sighed and checked his watch. Luminous dials. Expensive watch. 'It's three a.m. British time, or midday Australian. Take your pick.'

It didn't feel like either.

Tessa struggled with the sense that she was dreaming, blinked, blinked again, and then the lights came on.

'Damn,' the deep voice said mournfully. 'My prediction was wrong. Now you won't think me a seasoned traveller.'

'Are you one?' Tess asked cautiously. The man looked like a farmer. He didn't come across as someone who flitted frequently around the world on business.

'Yep. I fly from Warrnambie to Melbourne once a month, rain or shine.'

Tess thought this through.

'You mean—Warrnambie, Victoria, Australia, to Melbourne, Victoria, Australia? A distance of about a hundred miles?'

'That's right.' His smile told her she was a clever girl. As if he were humouring her instead of the other way around.

'That makes you a seasoned traveller?'

'Hey, I've been to England before,' he told her, wounded. 'But not once a month. Mostly because I don't like aeroplane breakfasts.' He yawned and stretched, his big frame touching her shoulder as he moved. The warmth from his body seemed to flow straight through the blankets and into hers.

'So...' Tess was making a Herculean effort to keep the conversation sane. This man had organized her a seat and lent her a shoulder. She had to be nice, no matter how breathless he made her feel. 'So you live at Warrnambie?'

'That's where my farm is.' He was interrupted by the hostess. A moist, warm towel was handed to each of them, held aloft with a pair of silver tongs. Tessa's companion disappeared under his white towel for a minute or two, rubbing himself down with the enjoyment of a bear under a waterfall. Then he emerged to redirect his attention to Tess. 'That's better. A shave and I'll almost be up to introductions. Don't go away.'

He stretched his large frame into an upright position and disappeared toward the rest room. Tess was left staring blankly after him, wondering just what it was that made the world seem to hold its breath in this man's presence.

In fact, it was an hour and breakfast later before they finally got around to introductions, and by that time Tess was almost starting to feel human. She'd washed, repaired the worst of the ravages to her face and, despite her companion's disparagement of airline food, managed to put away a decent breakfast. It was the first full meal she could remember eating since she'd heard about Christine's death, and she hadn't realized just how hungry she was.

Charles watched her with growing concern.

'You don't say you *like* this stuff?' he demanded, prodding an omelette which bore a strong resemblance to a piece of bath foam. 'The hens that laid these eggs have serious problems. I think they've been fed a diet of rubber pellets and orange cordial.'

Tess chuckled, and was faintly astonished at the sound. That she could laugh…

Charlie Cameron's smile broadened.

'Now, how did I know it'd sound like that?' he said approvingly. 'The very nicest chuckle…' He held out his hand and took hers, enveloping her fingers in a strong, warm clasp. 'Allow me to repeat my proposal. I've been through all the papers and there's nothing else for it. You'll just have to marry me.'

'Don't be...' Tessa tried unsuccessfully to draw her hand away. 'Don't be silly,' she said nervously, glancing up to see just where the hostess was, just in case she needed help to haul off a deranged and disappointed lunatic. 'You don't even know me.'

'I know enough. You're not wearing a wedding ring and you have the nicest chuckle I've ever had the privilege of hearing,' Charles said. 'And when we stopped at Singapore and the old Indian lady dropped her baggage, you were the one who got down on her hands and knees and hauled it back together.' He noted her look of surprise and smiled again. 'I was in the business class lounge or I would have dashed to the rescue myself—as befits my status as hero and husband material—but I could see what happened through the glass,' he added. 'That'll do as an introduction.'

'Well, I don't know you,' Tessa said breathlessly. 'For heaven's sake, this is ridiculous. I don't know you from Adam and you're asking me to marry you?'

'I know you. I've read your baggage labels. Tessa Flanagan, and a very nice name too. Tessa Cameron sounds better. But I guess you don't know me.' Charles considered. And then he frowned. 'I have a problem here,' he confessed. 'I'm not really sure yet who I am.'

'You're not sure?' Tessa glared. This was getting crazier and crazier. 'What do you mean—you're not sure?'

'Well, I think I'm sure,' he told her, and smiled apologetically. 'Until a week ago, I was Charles Cameron, cattle farmer from Warrnambie.'

'And now?'

'Well...' He sighed. Then he lifted up one of the papers he'd been studying. 'According to this, I'm Lord

Charles Cameron, thirteenth Earl of Dalston. Owner of a grand-sounding title, and—if you'll agree to marry me—owner of one rather decrepit castle and all it contains.'

CHAPTER TWO

VERY little was said for the next hour until they came in to land at Heathrow. Too much had happened to Tess for her to continue humouring this nutcase. She was polite—but only just.

'I'm very pleased you're going to be an earl,' she told him, 'but it has absolutely nothing to do with me. If you don't mind, I want to read. Go back to your papers and figure out how you can inherit your castle all by yourself.'

She turned her shoulder resolutely away, and ignored him.

Charles Cameron didn't ignore her. He delved back into his documents but she was aware of him silently watching her out of the corner of his eye.

Drat the man! He threw her right off balance and she had to concentrate.

Tess had a folder full of travel documents given to her by the agent in Yaldara Bay. And instructions that scared the life out of someone who'd travelled three times to Sydney for her nursing exams and that was as far from home as she'd ever been.

Now...she had to go through Customs in Heathrow, find the Airbus office, catch the bus to the coach station—then walk about five blocks to the cheap bed and breakfast the agent had booked for her. She had a map. It was all here. Just follow the instructions.

'I'm being met by a driver,' Charles said in her ear and made her jump. 'I can give you a lift.'

'I don't want a lift,' Tessa said crossly. 'Thank you. My bus fare is paid.'

'Very efficient.' Charles lifted her travel documents and frowned down at the page of instructions telling her where to go. 'Backblow Street. I don't know about my future wife staying here.'

'Well, you go and ask your future wife where she wants to stay,' Tessa managed. 'Just leave me alone.'

'But...'

'No,' she said flatly. 'Please...just leave me be.'

They parted soon after landing.

Charles somehow managed to stay by her side until they hit the queue for Immigration. Then there were two queues—one for British subjects and one for aliens. To her surprise, Charles headed for the local queue.

'I'll wait for you on the other side,' he said, but she shook her head resolutely. Her passage through was surprisingly swift; her luggage was the first off the conveyor belt and then she was at the Airbus terminal knowing she need never see Charlie Cameron again in her life.

She should be relieved. She should be shaking off the memory of such a lunatic with speed. Instead, she boarded her bus feeling as desolate as she'd ever felt in her life.

It must be Christine's death, she told herself, and the fact that she was on the other side of the world from Donald. From anyone she knew.

But as she sat on the top of her double-decker bus, heading for central London, the thought of Charlie Cameron's gentle smile stayed with her.

He was a nut but a nice nut, she decided as she buried herself in the map showing her where to go when she left the bus. She could afford to remember him with affection.

But a tiny voice at the back of her head told her she didn't want to remember him at all. The thought of his strong arm around her—the feel of his cashmere sweater—the sheer maleness of the man—that was what she wanted.

Oh, yeah? And the thought of being wife to the Earl of Dalston? she told herself grimly. If he's the Earl of Dalston then I'm travelling on a flying pig. Now stop thinking about lunatics and start thinking about maps.

It took Tess an hour to find her hotel and by the time she did it was still only seven in the morning and she was exhausted.

Donald had presented her with a set of baggage wheels as a farewell present. 'Because taxi prices are sky high and you'll be using enough of our house savings as it is,' he'd told her. 'Using these wheels, you can walk pulling your things behind you. They'll make you independent.'

Which they might have if they'd been good quality, Tess thought grimly. The streets were rough and the plastic wheels were weak. Tess walked a block before the first wheel buckled. Then she was left with no choice but to carry everything by hand. There wasn't even a rubbish bin where she could dump her broken wheels. She had to carry them as well.

It was the middle of June. At home it had been crisp and cool in the beginning of winter. Here it was summer. It was too early to be hot but it was humid enough to be uncomfortable, and Tessa's jogging suit was way too heavy. By the time she stopped outside a dubious-looking lodging house, she was exhausted.

At least she'd made it. Primrose Place. Bed and breakfast.

Tess looked up at her lodgings with dismay. She had to stay in London for a couple of nights—she needed to see her sister's lawyer before she went north—and accommodation in the city was expensive. Donald and the travel agent had chosen this place for her from a brochure. Surely it hadn't looked like this in the advertisement?

The place looked just plain seedy. The last primrose to grace Primrose Place had hoisted its roots and departed centuries ago, breathing a sigh of relief as it did. All that was left was a dingy, soot-covered building. The cracked window in the front was plastered with newspaper, and a smell of stale grease hung about the front door.

She had no choice. She had to stay here. Her accommodation was paid.

Tess looked up and down the street. All the buildings here— a long line of terraces three storeys high—were much the same, all slightly unkempt and grubby. The street was early-morning quiet, milk bottles standing empty on each doorstep. A large black car nosed its way into the end of the street and stopped, its engine still running. Its occupants didn't emerge.

This was like something out of a second-rate whodunnit movie.

Maybe it was because she was very much alone that she felt uneasy. Despite the heat, Tess shivered, and rang the bell fast.

The bell echoed hollowly inside, and she heard a mass of dog flesh hurling itself against the other side of the door. Hardly a welcome. All she heard was snarling.

The snarling ended with a human curse and then the door opened. Her landlord stood before her, still in the bottom half of dirty pyjamas, bald, unshaven and his flabby white chest bare.

'What d'ya want?'

Tess caught her breath.

'I'm...I'm booked in here.' She held out her accommodation voucher. The man took it, kicked the dog back from behind him and sniffed as he inspected it. Then he thrust the voucher back at her.

'This is for tonight. Come back five o'clock when the doors open. Not before.' And he slammed the door in her face.

Tess hadn't cried. Not once. Not when the phone call had come telling her Christine was dead. Not when Christine's mother-in-law had told her she was crazy to come and she wasn't wanted. Not when she'd said goodbye to Donald.

She came very close now.

She stood on the greasy doorstep and took great lungfuls of humid air and fought for control. It was seven o'clock in the morning in a strange city and she had nowhere to go.

A hand landed on her shoulder and held.

Tess yelped. There was no other word to describe the sound that came out as she jumped about six inches in the air. When she came down to land, the hand was still on her shoulder, turning her around to face whoever it was accosting her.

But Tessa Flanagan was no victim. As charge nurse at Yaldara Bay Hospital, Tessa's reactions to emergencies were tuned to be lighting-swift—and now was no exception.

She attacked right back.

During one very boring winter in Yaldara Bay, Tess had enrolled in a self-defence course for women. Then, after an incident with a drunk in Casualty, she'd taught the same class to the junior nurses on her staff. Over and over.

Sometimes she'd wondered whether it really would work. If she was attacked, would she be so frightened that she'd freeze?

Obviously not. Her training worked a treat.

As her attacker hauled her around to face him—before she even saw who was attacking—she thumped her fist fair across his left eye. In the same instant, Tessa's spare hand dropped and came upward fast, crunching as hard as she possibly could. Right into his private parts.

And Charlie Cameron grunted in agony, fell back and clutched himself where it hurt most.

Tess stared…and stared some more.

'Charlie…'

'So who were you expecting?' Charlie managed, groaning and bent double. 'Jack the Ripper? Hell, Tess, you've damaged me for life!'

'But…'

'You'll have to marry me now. I'm damaged goods. You can't return me.'

Charlie. Charlie, the Earl of Dalston. Charlie, the lunatic.

It was too much. It was all too much. Tess stared down, appalled, and the world spun around her. And finally, after all this time, the tears came.

'Oh, Charlie, I'm so sorry…'

Charlie straightened and stared. 'Tess…what's going on here? You hit me where it hurts most and *you* cry!'

'I don't cry. I never cry.' It was as much as Tessa could do to make her voice work through her tears.

'Yeah? And I'm Peter Pan.' He groaned again. 'Come to think of it, I might be. Isn't Peter Pan the boy who can't grow up? Any minute now I'll be back to singing soprano.' He winced again. He shook his head. 'I don't believe this. You've interrupted the succession of the Dalston line with one fell fist, you've given me a black eye and *you* cry...'

Tessa didn't stop. She couldn't. And Charlie, the Earl of Dalston, pulled himself together. He groaned again, but in resignation. Somehow he made it up the steps to haul her in against his broad shoulders, and Tess wept and wept against Charlie-the-lunatic's shirt for all of two minutes.

She soaked him. Tessa's tears made a sodden circle against his shoulder, and she didn't stop howling until the shirt fabric was almost transparent and she could feel the warmth of his skin underneath her cheek.

Somehow she took a ragged breath and pulled away. Charlie allowed her room to back twelve inches, but his hands held her shoulders, his face creased in concern.

'I...I'm so sorry,' she managed finally. 'Really...I don't cry.'

'I can see that,' he said approvingly and gave her a wry smile. 'It's another reason I've decided you should marry me. Apart from needing you for self-defence. Some of us earls employ bodyguards. I'll just keep you around. Here. Have a handkerchief.'

There was nothing to say to that. She really did need that handkerchief.

'Blow,' Charlie told her. 'And before you ask, I don't want it back.' His smile deepened. 'One thing I've decided about being an earl, I can afford to be generous with my handkerchiefs.'

Tess sniffed, gave a watery chuckle—and blew. And blew again, while Charlie smiled down at her in gentle concern.

'Better?'

'Better.' Tess emerged from his linen and gave him a wavering smile. 'I'm sorry. What you must think...' Her smile faded. 'Oh, Charlie, your eye…' She stared up at him with guilt. 'It's changing colour already.'

Charlie fingered his bruised face and winced. 'No matter,' he said nobly. And winced again. 'They say you only feel one pain centre at a time and they're right. Your other area of attack is of more concern. Hell, Tess, what did you think you were doing?'

'Defending myself,' she told him, indignation flooding back as she saw the twinkle in his eyes. Drat the man, was he never serious? She looked down the street to where the sleek black car—a Jaguar—was waiting by the kerb. 'It was *you* in the car,' she said accusingly. 'Waiting in the street like a gangster. You scared me to death!'

'Yeah, well, you're not showing any long-term damage.' Charlie managed another heartfelt groan. 'Whereas I just may start singing falsetto. Besides, I thought it was your friend in the hotel who scared you,' he said mildly. 'Your friend with the sexy pyjamas.'

'You saw.' Tessa was so confused that for a minute she forgot this man was a nutcase. She thought of the pyjamas in question and gave another tearful chuckle. 'Oh, isn't he awful? I can't stay here.'

'No. You can't stay here.' Charlie's hands came back to grip her shoulders. 'That's what I was trying to tell you on the plane. You wouldn't listen. This address is seedy and this hotel has to be the seediest in the district.'

'But…' Tess took a ragged breath and steadied. And pulled away from his hands. 'Charlie, I've paid for it. I can't…'

'You can't have paid very much.'

'We didn't. But Donald says…'

'Donald?'

'My fiancé.'

Silence.

My fiancé. The word echoed in the silence of the street and Tess bit her lip. She'd had to say it, though. It wouldn't do this man any harm to know there was a man in her life. A man who cared for her. But Charlie's eyes were snapping down in a frown. He hauled up her ring finger and held it in the sunlight for inspection.

'No ring,' he said accusingly.

'I don't have to wear a ring,' she told him, her voice just a trace unsteady.

'It'd help. When a man's looking out for a bride under desperate circumstances...'

'You mean a man like you.'

'Yes. A man who needs to be married.'

'He wants a sign, I suppose.' Tess glared. 'I'm sorry, Mr Cameron, but I don't see why I should wear "claimed" labels just for you.'

'Doesn't Donald believe in diamonds?'

'We're saving for a house,' Tess said with asperity. She was back under control now, and growing more indignant by the minute. 'Now, if you've finished the inquisition...'

'If you were my fiancée, I'd make sure you were wearing a diamond so large every other man could see it for miles,' Charlie told her. 'I'd be so proud. You're gorgeous, you're kind, and you're a warrior maiden to boot. I'd buy you an engagement ring before any bricks and mortar.'

'Even a castle?' Tess said before she could help herself, and Charlie had the temerity to grin.

'Well, who knows? What price a castle?' And then he leaned over and lifted her baggage. 'Hell. This weighs a ton. We saw you walk into the street. *Walk!* What the hell were you doing walking instead of taking a cab?' And then he sighed and held up a hand. 'No. Don't tell me. I know. Donald and his house saving. You know,

I've decided to take no notice of Donald. You mock my castle and I'll mock your Donald. Until the man comes charging to rescue you, bearing diamonds, he can be set aside of no import. I've decided, Tessa Flanagan, that you need a hero, and I'm it.'

'I don't need anything of the kind.'

'How about an earl?'

'I especially don't need an earl.'

'Well, how about a simple farmer from home?' Charlie's voice suddenly gentled and the eyes looking down at her were warm and direct. 'A farmer with a flat in Belgravia, very close to here. It's a flat with four bedrooms, one of which is a guest suite.' And then, as Tessa's face froze, he smiled and shook his head. 'And yes, my intentions are far from honourable, but I'll respect the horrid Donald by making you a promise. You'll be absolutely safe from all harm in my house, Tessa Flanagan, for however long you stay.'

And he made a signal to the man behind the wheel of the car. The lid of the car's luggage compartment flipped up and he heaved Tessa's bag into it.

'But...I'm not coming with you,' Tessa stammered.

'Where are you going, then?'

'I don't know. Anywhere!' Tess looked wildly around the deserted street, but there were no warm and welcoming little cafés within sight. No more hotels. Nowhere she could go and dump her gear.

So what would she do? Would she sit on her suitcase right here and wait until five o'clock? Or drag her belongings along to Christine's lawyer?'

Charlie watched the doubts flit across her face and he lifted a hand and touched Tessa's cheek with a gentle finger.

'There's little choice here, Tess,' he said softly. 'You can trust me. I swear.'

Tess looked up at him. His eyes were crinkled and kind and absolutely direct.

'I don't trust you. How can I? You're nuts,' she managed. 'Do you really have a flat in London?'

'I really do and it's quite close,' he assured her.

'And it's yours?' she asked.

'It was my uncle's. Now it seems that it's mine.'

Tess bit her lip. 'That must mean your uncle, the twelfth earl.'

'Clever girl,' he said approvingly. 'You've worked out the family tree. Now...do you want to trust me?'

Tessa didn't. She badly didn't want to trust him. There was something about Charlie Cameron that said she should steer as far away from this man as possible. Lunatic or not, he left her feeling as if her feet weren't quite steady on the ground.

But the street was sordid and empty, her baggage was heavy and her feet hurt. There were blisters on her palms from carrying the weight this far.

And this man was her only link with home.

What was the worst that could happen here? That he take her to this imaginary castle, lock her with his harem of slaves and keep her for his own personal pleasure?

She looked back at her hotel and her creepy landlord was peering over the newspaper in the front window. He was scratching his flabby white chest and scowling, and she just knew that any minute he'd rush out and order her off his filthy front step, or set the dog on her.

She looked up at Charlie and her fear receded. Maybe there was something to be said for harems, after all.

Charlie's house wasn't quite a harem but it was a lot closer to a palace than anywhere Tess had ever been before. She'd sat silently in the rear seat of the Jaguar while the driver negotiated London's early-morning traffic, and ten minutes later they had pulled up outside a place Tess could only describe as a mansion.

She gazed out in astonishment. The house was gleaming white stone, three storeys high, with Gothic columns at the entrance and a vast, overwhelming front door.

'Before you get the wrong idea, only the top floor's mine,' Charlie said quickly, seeing her jaw drop. 'And there's no garden. We use the square over the road.'

The square. Tessa turned to see. On the other side of the road was a park, filled with mature trees, lush green lawns and immaculately groomed gardens.

'There's ten houses with access,' Charlie said apologetically. 'We have to share.'

'Oh, poor you,' Tess managed.

'We bear it,' Charlie told her, and he grinned. 'We earls live in hard times. Come on in. Henry will bring in our gear.'

Henry. Tess looked doubtfully at the man in the front seat. He was in his sixties, dapper and trim and dressed in a chauffeur's uniform. Henry hadn't said a word the whole time she'd been in the car.

'This isn't a hire car?' she asked cautiously.

'Well, no. I guess it's mine. Or it might be mine.'

'Might?'

Charlie spread his hands. 'Tess, this is my uncle's home, my uncle's chauffeur, my uncle's lifestyle. He's left it all to me—conditionally.'

'Conditionally?'

'On me being married by the time I'm thirty,' Charlie told her. 'That's in six weeks. So you see why I'm so interested in ladies who don't sport engagement rings?' And he gave her his most engaging smile. 'Now, are you coming into my parlour, *said the spider to the fly*, or am I leaving you to London's tender mercies out here on the street?'

He slid his long form out of the car.

There was nothing for Tessa to do but to follow.

The house was as breathtaking as its façade.

The entrance hall was vast, and the lift whisked them to the third floor in silent opulence. The lift was bigger than Tessa's bedroom at home. Tess was almost too flummoxed to speak.

The lift drew to a silent halt, the doors slid wide and Charlie Cameron was welcomed to his world.

'Mr Charlie!' A stout lady, aproned, motherly and beaming goodwill, bustled forward to greet Charlie before he'd stepped out of the lift. 'Oh, it's so good to have you home.' And she enveloped as much as she could of him in an enormous bear hug.

To which Charlie responded in kind. He lifted the little lady high, swung her round so her feet didn't touch the floor, kissed her soundly and then set her down on the marble tiles. He grinned down at her dimply figure and sighed.

'It's good to be here, Mary.' Then he turned to Tess. 'Mary, this is Miss Tessa Flanagan. Tessa, this is Mrs Henry Robertson but she only answers to Mary. Mary, Tessa's from home and she needs a bed. Henry and I found her stranded with her suitcase in Backblow Street and we couldn't just leave her there, now could we?'

Mary's bright eyes took in Tessa from the toes up. It was a fast, cursory glance, but it appeared Tess passed inspection. It seemed that this was no stately home with dress requirements to match.

'Oh, of course you couldn't,' Mary said warmly. 'Backblow Street? What on earth were you thinking of, letting your friends go there, Mr Charlie? It's a filthy place. Miss Tessa can have the blue room, if you think that's suitable.' Then she stared, for the first time focussing properly on Charlie. 'Mr Charlie, what on earth have you done to your face?'

'It's a modern equivalent to a love bite,' Charlie told her, grinning wickedly at Tess. 'And that's not the half of it, Mary. If I told you the full damage, you'd be shocked to the core. Just look after Tess and don't give her any lip.'

Mary's eyes widened. She looked from Tess to Charlie and back again—but finally decided she wouldn't get anywhere with enquiries. She obviously knew Charlie well.

She shrugged and smiled. 'Well, no matter. You're always getting yourself into some scrape or another, Mr Charlie. Now, would you like time to wash before you have breakfast?' she asked Tess. Once again, that kindly, perceptive appraisal. 'Oh, of course you would, child. In fact, what you look like you need, Miss Tessa, if you won't take this personally as I'm sure you won't, is a long, hot bath, up to your neck in bubbles. Does that sound good?'

Good. Good!

Tessa's face said it all, and Charlie chuckled behind her. 'Take her away, Mary, and soak her. I'll look after myself.' He turned away to go left down the hall but Mary stopped him with a hand on his arm.

'I've put you in your uncle's room,' she said softly, watching his face. 'I thought...'

Charlie's smile faded. He stood looking down at Mary for a long, long moment. Then he sighed.

'This is going to be hard, Mary.'

'It is.'

Charlie closed his eyes. When he opened them, his face was grim. The twinkle had disappeared entirely.

'Very well,' he said. 'Let's start this now.'

* * *

Tessa's bath was glorious. The bedroom itself was sumptuous, with plush white carpet, a vast, canopied bed and blue and gold curtains over a wall of windows which looked over the square and the rooftops of London beyond.

The *en suite* bathroom had the same fantastic view, and the bath—which could have accommodated three of Tessa—was amazing.

'It's a shame to bathe at night because you need to close the curtains or turn off the light if you're not to shock the neighbours,' Mary told her as she handed her an armload of bath towels. 'But the good thing about English summer is our lack of night-time. Enjoy your bath, lass.' And she left her to soak.

Tess soaked. And soaked.

It was the first quiet time Tess had had since she'd heard of Christine's death. It was the first time her responsibilities and need for organization had eased. The shadow of Christine's death receded, with the image of Charles Cameron superimposing itself on her thoughts. Tess lay back under the foam, stared up at the ornate plasterwork on the high ceiling and wondered just what she had got herself into.

The image of Charlie Cameron as a lunatic was fading. Henry and the maternal, perceptive Mary seemed dependable and trustworthy, and they formed a respectable backdrop for the man. Tess was almost starting to believe in the earldom. And the castle. Almost.

'Surely he doesn't seriously expect to get married in six weeks?' she asked the ceiling. 'But then...to lose all this if he doesn't...'

It was too hard. She drifted in and out of her bubbly haze until Mary's call pulled her back to reality.

'That bathwater'll be getting cold, lass. You pull on a bathrobe and come for breakfast.'

A bathrobe.

Tess looked about her warily. She didn't want to put on her soiled jogging suit again but…

There was a thick white bathrobe hanging from the door. Tess towelled herself dry and examined it with caution.

It was a gorgeous garment. It wrapped completely around her with heaps to spare and came down to her toes. The white towelling was absolutely plain except for a rich purple letter embroidered on the breast pocket.

'D'.

D for Dalston?

If this was all a hoax then it was some elaborate set-up, Tess decided. But…Charlie as an earl? Charles Cameron wasn't like any earl Tess had ever met.

Tess made a silly face at herself in the mirror, grabbed a comb from her handbag and attacked her washed and tangled curls with force.

Yeah, well, exactly how many earls have you met before, Tessa Flanagan? she asked herself. Heaps and heaps? Or only one? An earl called Charlie. And he's waiting for you at breakfast. So put some clothes on and go and find him.

Easier said than done. Her clothing had disappeared. Tess came cautiously out into her bedroom to find no sign of her baggage.

There was a pair of soft, fit-all slippers by the bed—also engraved with D. Tess slid them on and padded out into the hall. She was feeling stranger and stranger.

As if she really were in a harem.

'Any minute now a slave or two will pop out, perfume me and cart me off to the master,' she said grimly.

'Hey, I'd like that!'

Tess swung around like a scalded cat. Charlie was

standing at the door of the room opposite, dressed in a bathrobe identical to hers.

The master himself. And he'd heard what she had said.

Tess blushed scarlet from the toes up.

'You don't need a slave to perfume you. You look cuter than I do in that thing,' Charlie complained, ignoring her blush. 'It isn't fair.'

She might look cuter—but Charlie looked staggeringly male. Charles might be wearing an identical bathrobe to Tessa's, but on him it looked completely different. The robe only came to Charlie's knees. His brown legs emerged beneath like solid trunks.

Because the robe didn't have quite the capacity to wrap round Charlie's much larger body, his chest was bare to the waist. His chest was tanned, muscled and coated with deep black hair—just like the hair on his head which, wet from his shower or bath, was clinging in damp tendrils across his brow. The strands were just touching the bruise across his eye. Tess hauled back on an almost irresistible urge to brush the strands back. To soothe the hurt...

Ridiculous! She kept her hands strictly to herself.

'I...I couldn't find my clothes.'

'Nor I, mine. If I know Mary, we'll get them cleaned and pressed whether we want them cleaned and pressed or not.' Charlie grinned his slow, lazy smile that did funny things to Tessa's insides. 'Last time I came here I brought my Drizabone—the coat I use for mustering cattle back home. It's useful when I go up north and don't want to stay indoors. Mary attacked it with force. When I got back to Australia, I was the only cattleman in the country wearing a Drizabone with a starched collar!'

Tessa's strain eased as the image made her grin.

Drizabones were standard wear for Australian farmers—huge, brown waterproof coats that were only valued after they'd been worn in by hard work and grime. To wash one was almost sacrilege. And to starch it...

Charlie chuckled with her and the strain eased some more.

There was a wonderful smell wafting from the end of the hall and Charles was leading her toward it. He held open the door for Tess to precede him, and she brushed against his long body as she passed. Towelling against towelling...

He was so big and so male and... And his feet and legs were bare. And the strain came flooding back! Tess was having all sorts of irrelevant thoughts about what would happen as those bare legs stretched upward...

Good grief! The way she was thinking she almost deserved to be a slave. *And* she was engaged to Donald!

She fought her mounting colour and tried to concentrate on what was before her. That wasn't hard. The dining table was groaning under a pile of food.

The table itself was vast, built to seat a dozen or more. The room was ornate and gilt and...

'And too damned formal for words,' Charlie growled. 'What's wrong with the kitchen, Mary?'

'You know you only use the kitchen when you come here by yourself,' Mary told him. 'Your uncle always uses...used...the dining room.'

'Well, that's one way I don't have to follow in his footsteps.' Charlie pushed open the double doors. Beyond the dining room lay a kitchen, warm and fragrant with cooking, the vast Aga stove along the far wall a welcome in itself. Infinitely more comfortable than the ornate dining room. 'We'll eat in here.'

'But I'm baking bread.'

'Then Tess and I will watch you bake as we eat. Not

that you need to bake for weeks by the look of this lot.' He lifted a plate from the table and sniffed in delight. 'Singing hinnies. Mary, now I know I'm back.'

'Home,' Mary said softly. 'You're home, my lord. Where you belong.'

'Mary...'

'Your place is right here now,' she told him and her voice grew a little stern, as though she were a nanny reminding a child of his duty. 'You're the Earl of Dalston now, my lord. Whether you like it or not.'

CHAPTER THREE

'SO TELL me how you come to be an Australian earl?' Tess asked over her second cup of coffee. To her surprise, she'd packed away another vast breakfast.

'I told you you shouldn't have eaten the airline breakfast,' Charlie had told her as she'd looked at her loaded plate in dismay, but in the end it hadn't made any difference at all. She had been making up for lost time. Now Mary had whisked herself off to supervise unpacking and they were left alone.

It felt weird. It was eleven in the morning and she was sitting in a bathrobe over breakfast with the Earl of Dalston.

With Charlie.

'You've already figured it,' Charlie told her. 'My uncle died without issue.'

'Issue?'

'Kids.' He grinned. 'Toe-rags. Noisy little blighters who spend all your money. My uncle could never abide them. Or women either. He romanticized marriage—he thought every man should have a wife—but he was too lousy to get one for himself. Even sharing the toothpaste would have made him wince.'

'He and your father were brothers?'

'Yep. They were as unalike as two men could be, but brothers for all that.' Charlie poured himself another coffee and leaned back. 'As soon as he came of age, Dad took his share of the family fortune and set himself up on a farm in Australia. He married my mom—an American girl—and my uncle decided then that we were completely beyond the pale. Dad died two years ago, without ever having come back to the old country.'

'I'm sorry.'

'Don't be.' Charlie smiled. 'My father had a better life than my uncle ever had. He and my mom were very much in love. He died just a few months after she did, and neither of them regretted a thing about their lives. Except maybe not having more children.'

'There's only you?'

'Yep.'

Tess nodded, thinking it through. 'But...if your father hasn't been back...how come you've been here?'

'I was heir to the earldom,' Charlie said simply. 'My father always knew my uncle wouldn't marry and my mom and dad taught me what to expect early. They sent me over to stay with my grandparents.'

'Your grandparents?'

'My grandfather was the eleventh earl,' Charlie told her. 'He died eight years ago. He and I were best of friends. It was only my uncle who couldn't bear the thought that I'd inherit.'

'Why?'

'I broke a Dresden vase when I was nine years old.' Charlie's lazy grin flashed out again—magnetic and intense. 'The dogs and I were chasing my uncle's cat at the time. A fatter, lazier cat you've never seen and I let my grandfather's hounds into the house, just to stir her. I don't think my uncle ever forgave me. He thought I was a wastrel and a scoundrel. And totally useless at taking on responsibilities.'

'And a wife is supposed to cure all that?'

Charlie's eyes widened. 'Of course,' he said blandly. 'How can it not? If you take me on, how can I help but turn into the epitome of steadiness and sober duty?'

'It doesn't sound much fun,' Tessa said doubtfully, considering. 'Steadiness and sober duty.'

'With you it would be.'

'Charlie...' Tessa's colour mounted again. 'Don't!'

'Because of Donald?'

'Yes, because of Donald,' she snapped. 'And a thousand other reasons. The idea is totally crazy.' She pushed back her cup. 'Now...I need to find my clothes.' She glanced at her watch. 'I have an appointment this afternoon somewhere in Kensington. I don't know where that is and I need to find it.'

'It's ten minutes' walk from here.'

'Really?'

'Well, it depends whereabouts in Kensington, but fifteen minutes at the outside.' Charlie's eyes didn't leave hers. 'I can take you there if you need me.'

'I don't. Thank you.' Good grief, she had to start being independent soon.

'And you're not going to tell me what the appointment is?'

'There's no need.'

'No need to tell me?'

He was watching her with that calm kindness of his—the kindness that could be her undoing. The kindness that made her want to place all her cares on his broad shoulders. Which was ridiculous. She was an independent woman. Tessa's mother had been ill for years and Tess had taken over family responsibilities early. She was a trained nurse in charge of a small hospital. She was competent to fight her own battles.

But, independent or not, maybe Charles Cameron deserved to be told why she was floundering here. After all, he was giving her free accommodation. Even Donald would tell her to be grateful.

So she told him.

'I have an appointment with my sister's lawyer,' she said slowly, the pain in her voice impossible to conceal. 'My sister and her husband died last week in a car crash just north of London. My sister's husband is English and they lived here. The funeral was five days ago. I've just come over to...' Her voice faltered to a halt.

'To say goodbye?' Charlie said softly and Tessa's eyes flew to his face.

'I suppose you think that's stupid.'

'I don't think anything of the kind.' Charlie's large hand came over the table and gripped hers. And held. 'When my grandfather died I was in America with my mom's people and didn't hear of his death for two weeks. My uncle saw no need to contact me. But when I heard...I had to come. Just to stand by his grave and say what I had to say.'

Tess blinked. And blinked again.

'I'm not going to cry,' she said.

'No. Of course you're not.' Charlie cupped her chin in his fingers and tilted her face so she was looking at him. 'You're the bravest...'

'I am not!' Tess shoved her chair back and rose. 'And if you keep this up, I will cry again and it serves you right if I do.'

'I agree.'

'I don't want you to agree,' she said crossly. 'I want you to tell me I'm stupid like everyone else does.'

'Like Donald? Does Donald tell you you're stupid?'

She retreated and glowered and Charlie laughed and held up his hands in surrender.

'Okay. Okay. I won't sympathize any more and I won't cast any nasturtiums at Dreadful Donald. Tell me why we're going to see your sister's lawyer.'

'Not *we*.'

'We,' he said firmly. 'Now I know for certain that

you're a damsel in distress, my hero instinct won't be ignored. I refuse to let you battle lawyers on your own.'

'I'm not battling…'

'You always battle lawyers,' Charlie said in a voice of sage experience. 'Look at me. I'm marrying to escape 'em.'

'Charlie…'

'Tell me.'

Tess took a deep breath and counted to ten, fighting for control. Fighting to ignore Charlie's preposterous suggestion that she marry him.

'I just need…I need to find out where I stand with Ben,' she said.

'Ben? Another man?' He was gently teasing, but Charlie's eyes weren't teasing. They were probing and intelligent and…

And knowing, Tess thought. As if he could see the trouble written across her heart.

'Ben's my nephew,' she said stiffly. There was no laughter where Ben was concerned. 'He's three.'

'Christine's child?'

'Christine's child.'

'Oh, no.' The trouble in Tessa's face was mirrored in Charlie's eyes. 'He wasn't hurt?'

'No,' she said quickly. 'He's safe.'

'And he's with?'

'His grandmother. Christine's mother-in-law.'

'I see.' Charlie leaned back in his chair. 'And you're going to see the lawyers because—'

'Because I need to know whether I can get access if Mrs Blainey refuses to let me see him,' Tess said slowly, thinking it through as she spoke. 'Mrs Blainey—my sister's mother-in-law and Ben's grandmother—didn't want me to come. She says it'll upset Ben. You see, Christine and I are twins. I look like…'

She faltered to a halt.

'You look like Christine,' Charlie finished for her. 'But you've come anyway and you still want to see Ben. I can understand that.'

'I can't get any answers from the laywer over the phone,' Tess said. 'I've only been able to make an appointment with the junior partner in the firm—not with the lawyer who acts for Christine. He also acts for Mrs Blainey, you see. But if I see him...he'll have to say whether I have a legal right to see Ben. '

'If he can't then I have an excellent lawyer who can find out for us,' Charlie said. 'I'll even put aside my aversion to lawyers in the cause.' He rose and crossed to her, and before she could stop him he took both her hands and squeezed them together in his. 'We'll resort to his advice together. But before we revert to such drastic measures as bringing in more legal eagles, let's see what we can do ourselves, Tess Flanagan. Together.'

Tess had been dreading her time with Christine's lawyer. The junior who'd spoken to her on the telephone had been supercilious and condescending.

'I'm sure Master Ben's well taken care of, Miss Flanagan. Mr Walter Scott's taking care of all the legal affairs of the estate. If you need any information, please write to this address.'

Mr Edward Scott, junior partner, had agreed to her request for an appointment with reluctance, and Tess had allowed herself two days in London in case of problems. She expected problems.

She hadn't counted on Charlie.

Charlie at her side, dressed to face city lawyers, was a presence indeed.

Tess wore a simple linen suit, soft blue and pressed into looking its best by Mary's careful ministration. Tess looked neat and presentable but not an imposing presence at all. Charlie made up for it.

Charles Cameron had stood out among the suits in business class in the aeroplane, and Tess had thought it was because he was wearing casual clothes. It was no such thing. In a dark, impeccably cut business suit, Charlie would turn just as many heads as he had in his moleskins. After a couple of hours on her wonderful bed, Tess emerged from her blue bedroom to find him waiting for her, and the sight of him just took her breath away.

The bruise on his eye had darkened but it took nothing from his appearance. Rather, it heightened the impression of strength, as if he'd just come from battle—victorious.

'You...you don't have to do this,' she managed, trying not to stare. 'I can go by myself.'

'I've put on a tie especially,' he said reproachfully. 'Don't quibble.'

That was the only protest she was allowed to make. Tess subsided and didn't quibble at all.

Scott, Scott and McPherson was a firm of lawyers of long standing. Henry drove Charles and Tess to a building steeped in history, and the worn brass plate outside said that whatever historic events had taken place here, Scott, Scott and McPherson had been around long enough to see them.

Tess took a deep breath, looking at the ancient stone lions guarding the portals. If this place had been purpose built to intimidate, it could scarcely have been more successful.

'Gird your loins here, lass,' Charlie said beside her. 'Together we can conquer anything—even lawyers.'

'What exactly does gird your loins mean?' Tess asked carefully, and Charlie chuckled.

'Whatever it is, I just bet you can't do it in pantyhose. Just don't let anyone push you around. I'm with you all the way.' He thrust the double doors wide and ushered her inside.

Tessa's reception was just as she had suspected it might be. Mr Edward Scott, junior partner, kept Tess and Charles waiting for twenty minutes in an outer waiting room that was as uncomfortable as it was austere. Finally he condescended to show them into his inner sanctum. His welcome was wintry. He sat them on two uncomfortable chairs and asked how he could help them in the tone of one who didn't expect to help them one bit.

Tess introduced Charles simply as Charles Cameron—for heaven's sake, what else was she to call him? The lawyer gave Charlie a long, assessing look, but Charles was keeping a low profile. He listened patiently while Tessa was effectively brushed aside as having nothing to do with her sister's affairs.

'As I told you on the telephone,' Mr Scott junior explained yet again, 'the estate is being looked after by Mr Scott senior and he's in the north at the moment.'

'But I'd like to see my nephew, and maybe have access to some of my sister's things,' Tess said meekly. 'There are family things... Christine and I were twins and...'

'All that will be sorted out when the estate is finalized. And as for having access, I believe Mrs Blainey has objected. She feels the family resemblance will unsettle the child.'

'You don't believe it might be good for Ben to know he has an aunt who loves him?' Charlie asked diffidently, and the lawyer flashed him a look of disdain.

'Mrs Blainey thinks not,' he said flatly. It was said as a statement not to be argued with.

'Well, I need to see Mrs Blainey face to face,' Tess managed. 'Christine gave me her telephone number some time ago, but I don't have her address. Could you at least give me that?'

'Mrs Blainey will give it to you if she sees fit. Telephone her and ask her.'

'I have.' Tess swallowed. 'She won't.'

'Then there's nothing more to be said.' The lawyer rose. The interview, it seemed, was over. 'I'm sorry, miss, if you've wasted your time coming to England, but I did warn you.'

'Just a moment.' Charlie hadn't moved. Now he brushed an imaginary speck of dust from his immaculate trousers and searched for more. 'We wish to see a copy of Mrs Blainey's will,' he said softly. 'Now.'

'I beg your pardon?' The lawyer's face showed astonishment. 'Mrs Blainey's not dead.'

Charlie sighed as if the man was being obtuse and gave up hunting for dust on his trousers. 'I meant Mrs Blainey junior, of course. Christine. Tessa's sister.' He looked up and met the lawyer's eyes and his face was implacable.

'We have the right to see her will,' he said flatly. 'I understand Christine's husband was killed instantly in the car accident and Christine died some twelve hours later. My lawyer tells me that anything her husband left her is therefore Christine's to dispose of. As Tessa is Christine's twin sister and Christine was a widow at the time of her death, it appears reasonable to believe something may be left to Tessa. The will was lodged in this office. We wish to see it.'

And he went back to dusting his trousers.

The lawyer stared down at Charlie for a long moment—and then he cleared his throat. All of a sudden he was uncomfortable. 'I believe Mr Scott Senior has taken the documents north with him,' he said.

'But you knew Miss Flanagan was coming here today.' There was an iciness in Charlie's voice that Tess hadn't heard before. His eyes swept up to meet the lawyer's. His look was flint and steel. 'Find her a copy,' he said. *'Now.'*

'I don't believe we can...'

'You can,' Charlie said. 'If Mr Scott senior, removed the only copy of the will when he knew Christine's sister was due here today, then he's been irresponsible to say the least. It's two on a Tuesday afternoon. I imagine Mr Scott senior is somewhere near a telephone. Contact him and get the will faxed here. We'll wait for as long as it takes.'

'I don't know whether I...'

'We're waiting,' Charlie said inexorably. 'Do it.'

'May I ask what rôle you have here?' the lawyer demanded, trying desperately to regain ascendancy. He stared at Charlie down his long, thin nose. His lawyer's stare was intended to disconcert but Charlie simply stared blandly back. Undeterred, the lawyer continued. 'I didn't catch your name. I believe if this is no business of yours then I must ask you to leave.'

'Oh, no, you don't,' Charles said softly. 'I don't know what game you're playing here, sport, but I don't intimidate as easily as that.' He rose and placed a hand on Tessa's shoulder. Pressed down with fingers that caressed as well as pressured. Sending tingles straight down to her toes and back again. But Charles was handing over his business card to the lawyer.

'This is who I am,' he said brusquely. 'Tessa's my affianced wife. We flew in together from Australia this morning and we intend to get some answers. And we want some answers. *Now!*'

Tess opened her mouth to speak—but no words came. Charles' hand on her shoulder was urgently insistent and the sensation from his fingers was numbing all by itself. Sit back and say nothing, the hand said, and Tessa's objections to what he'd just told the lawyer remained unvoiced.

The lawyer wasn't watching Tessa to see her astonishment. He was astonished enough himself. He glanced down at Charlie's business card and his jaw dropped a foot.

'Lord Dalston... You're *Lord Dalston*?' His voice was frankly incredulous. Another glance at Charlie and he appeared to change his mind. Disbelief faded. Charlie's bearing was every inch the aristocrat. 'I'm sorry, but...' He could barely stammer. 'Lord Dalston...'

'That's the one,' Charlie said pleasantly. 'And I have lawyers of my own. One of whom I contacted this morning to find out Tessa's rights. We're entitled to see the will, so run along and fetch a copy, my lad, or I'll have to instigate proceedings of my own. I don't know what delaying tactics Mrs Blainey senior has instructed your firm to use, but I'm quite sure they're illegal. Tessa's time in this country is short and if you waste it, then we'll sue for costs and for any unnecessary emotional hardship it might entail.' His lips twitched into a curve. 'And believe me, I'm just the person to help her do it.'

Charlie sat down again, his hand still warm on Tessa's shoulder, and he smiled up at the lawyer with a smile that Tess could only describe as dangerous. He crossed his legs, as though he was prepared to wait for what he needed—but not for very long. Not for very long at all.

'How did you know when my sister died?' It was all Tess could do to get her voice to work and it came out a squeak.

'I was curious,' Charlie told her blandly. The lawyer had left them alone and Tess had turned to Charles in astonishment. 'While you were having your nap after breakfast, I did some research. It wasn't hard to find the names of a couple killed in a motor accident a week ago. The details were in all the papers, including the fact that your sister died in a coma twelve hours after her husband.'

'I see.' Tess swallowed. 'Does that make a difference?'

'It might,' Charlie told her. 'Let's wait and see.' He frowned. 'I'm beginning to think the will might be interesting. They're going to such pains to keep it from you...'

'They're not keeping it. They've just taken it north...'

'But why?' Charles frowned. 'That's unusual. The original of a will should be kept in lawyers' vaults and only copies taken out of the office. Tess, would Mrs Blainey know you couldn't afford more than one trip to England?'

'She might,' Tess said doubtfully and then firmed. Her head was finally starting to work again. 'Yes, she would. Christine always bemoaned the fact that I couldn't afford to come over for the wedding or come and visit her.'

'So...if she wants to keep you from Ben, or whatever the will says you're entitled to, why not keep the will from you until after you return to Australia? That way, hopefully, you couldn't return to stake your claim.'

'But...why on earth would she do such a thing?'

'Let's wait and see what's in the will.'

It took Scott junior only ten minutes to get a copy of Christine's will. How he did, Tess neither knew nor cared. She took the document from the lawyer's hands and there was a long silence as she read through to the end.

When she finished, Tessa's face turned as white as chalk. She looked up at the lawyer. 'But this says...'

'I know what it says,' the lawyer said heavily. 'Mrs Blainey intends to appeal.'

'May I see?' Charlie leaned over and lifted the will from Tessa's nerveless fingers. He read it through to the end. And whistled.

'Good grief!'

Tessa closed her eyes. 'I don't believe it,' she said faintly. 'Why would Christine do something like this?'

'She must have had her reasons,' Charlie said softly. 'But whether you ever know what they are or not, you have some serious thinking to do.' He lifted the document and read aloud.

'In the event of my husband predeceasing me, then I bequeath all my worldly goods to my son, Benjamin, these possessions to be held in trust solely by my sister, Tessa Flanagan, to be used and administered at her sole discretion until Ben reaches twenty-one years of age. And, also in the event of my husband's death, I leave Ben's guardianship to my sister and ask that she take sole care of him.' Charlie paused.

Tessa was almost speechless. She shook her head, trying to clear the fog. 'Is it... Is this legally binding?'

'Mrs Christine Blainey didn't use our services to draft the will,' the lawyer said, in a tone that spoke of severe disapproval. 'If she had, we would have advised her most strongly against such a course of action. She lodged it with us in a sealed envelope. Clearly her husband's intention was not that all his possessions pass away from the family.'

'They're not passing from the family,' Charlie objected. 'They're passing to his son.'

'But they're moving out of his mother's control.'

'Is that such a crime?'

'I believe Mrs Blainey thinks so.' The lawyer hesitated and then relented a little. 'Mrs Blainey's a very determined lady.'

'I imagine she must be.' Charlie looked across at Tessa, his eyes speculative. 'Well, Tessa, what are you going to do about this?'

'Will Mrs Blainey fight the will?' Tess asked. 'Are there grounds?'

The lawyer looked from Charlie to Tessa and back again. Clearly he was coming to a decision. When Tess and Charles had walked into the room, this man had been loyal to a fault to the unknown Mrs Blainey. Now though... The lawyer's loyalties were shifting before their eyes, and Tess wondered just how much that had to do with Charlie's magic title.

'I believe her only grounds for legal action are that her son would not have wished Miss Flanagan to care for her grandchild,' the lawyer conceded. 'Her son's will didn't mention guardianship at all, but...'

The lawyer paused. Warring loyalties were plainly written on his face. Another glance at Charles and his mind was made up. 'I believe...if Mrs Blainey has the care of her grandson for a lengthy time, then she can apply to the courts for custody, saying it's in the child's best interests to stay with her long term. That hardly holds true now as the child's been with her for only a week, but it may be her idea in refusing access now.'

'She must want him very badly,' Tess said softly, her anger at the woman fading. She sighed. 'Maybe... If she loves him... She's his grandmother, after all. If Ben knows her and he's happy with her... Maybe he should stay with her.'

'That's up to you, miss,' the lawyer told her. 'I can't advise.' And then he took a deep breath and glanced at Charlie.

'But before you go... If you wish me to write down Mrs Blainey's address, I'll take it upon myself to do so.'

'So what are you going to do? Fly up north, pick up your nephew and take him back to Australia?'

Out in the busy London street everything looked the same as it had when they'd entered the lawyer's. Double-decker buses and square black London cabs drove past them, unconcerned that Tessa's life had just changed. She stood on the lawyer's front step and felt dizzy.

'I don't know.'

'Will you marry me?'

That shook her out of her trance. Tessa stared—and then gasped in indignation.

'No, I will not. And of all the nerve...to tell that lawyer that you were my fiancé...'

'He wouldn't have given you the address if I hadn't.'

'Well, that's even worse. And it's not true. He decided to be nice.'

'No, he didn't. He's a crawler,' Charlie said bluntly. 'Mrs Blainey's obviously a woman of influence and she persuaded her lawyers to act improperly. Our Mr Scott in there decided he didn't want to act improperly in the face of the Earl of Dalston. Not in the face of you or me, Tess, my love. In the face of my title.'

'I am *not* your love,' Tessa said angrily. 'And it stinks.'

'It does,' Charlie said calmly, taking her arm and leading her down the steps. 'But if I have a nice, lawyer-scaring title, then I might as well use it. Henry had these business cards made up for me and this is the first time I've used one.' He smiled. 'It's the very first time I've ever thought there might be something in this earl business.

'Well, earl or not, I'm not marrying you,' Tessa said crossly, ignoring his smile. 'I'm marrying Donald.'

'So what does Donald think about having Ben?'

'That's none of your business.'

'He doesn't want him?'

'I didn't say that.'

'You didn't need to. That'll make things interesting.'

'Look!' Tessa stopped dead and pulled herself away from Charlie's grasp. The pavement was busy. People were glancing curiously at them as they passed, but Tessa was unaware of their interest. Her head was spinning so fast she thought it could well spin off. 'All this is absolutely nothing to do with you,' she managed. 'Nothing! You've been very helpful, and I thank you, but from here on I'm on my own.'

'No, you're not,' Charlie said helpfully. 'You're not alone at all. Didn't you hear what the lawyer said? You've got Ben. And, of course,' he added blandly, 'you've got your Dreadful Donald.'

Tess pushed her hand up through her fair curls. She took three deep breaths. 'No,' she said at last. 'I don't have Ben. Regardless of what Christine wanted when she made her will, if it's better for Ben to stay with his grandmother then he can stay.'

'Is that what Donald thinks?'

'Oh, for heaven's sake! Will you be quiet?'

'Nope.' Charlie's smile broadened. 'It's not the job of us earls to be quiet. We've been sticking our noses into this country's business for generations.' Then, ignoring the dangerous spark of anger in Tessa's eyes, Charlie took her arm again and propelled her gently along the pavement. 'So...I take it you'll head off to Newcastle with speed?'

'Tomorrow,' Tess said, softening. 'I do need to check that Ben's okay and now I know her address in

Newcastle I can do that.' Then she looked doubtfully at the copy of the will the lawyer had given her. 'I guess, according to this, I need to go across to the Lake District and see to their house. Everything… I can't believe that Christine's left me everything.'

'Maybe her idea was that if Ben was left alone, you could live here—in her house—and care for him,' Charlie said gently. 'Depending on the house, it's not such a bad idea. The Lake District's lovely.'

'But that's crazy.'

'Because of Donald?'

'Because of Donald,' Tessa snapped. 'And besides, I'm an Australian. I can't live here.'

'Yes, you can.' Charlie pulled her arm tighter into his. 'But it'd make it much easier if you married an Englishman and made yourself right at home. An English earl, to be precise. And guess what?' He didn't give her a chance to answer but the twinkle in his dark eyes flashed out again, enmeshing her in his magnetic laughter.

'My castle's just north of the Lake District,' he said softly. 'Now, isn't that convenient?'

CHAPTER FOUR

THEY didn't go straight home. Charlie wouldn't hear of it.

'Nope. You've slept enough. You're telling me you're going north tomorrow. That means this is your only afternoon in London, it's your first time in England and it's my duty as an Englishman to see you make the most of it.

'You're not an Englishman.'

'I am,' he said, wounded. 'You ask Mary and Henry. They'll tell you. They've regarded my time in Australia and the States as holiday time and my American mom as someone nice but dotty and not to be taken seriously.' He glanced along the street and his eyes widened as he saw what was coming. 'Hey, I know what we can do.' Before Tessa could stop him, Charlie had put a hand in the air and a double-decker bus was pulling to a stop just near them.

Charlie took her hand and tugged her forward. 'Come on, Tess. This is great.'

'Where are we going?' Tess demanded, hauling back. 'Charlie…'

'I'm not abducting you,' Charlie told her. 'More's the pity. But this is a tourist bus built for sightseeing. Come on upstairs, my love, and let me show you London.'

The next three hours were time out.

The bus was almost empty when Charlie and Tess boarded. The top deck was open to the sky. Sitting in the front seat gave them a bird's-eye view of London, and there was nothing for Tessa to do but to sit back and enjoy it.

And she did. Despite the turmoil running through her head, somehow there seemed nothing to think about now but seeing London, with Charlie acting as a humorous and knowledgeable guide.

It was just plain wonderful. For Tess who'd been brought up with an English heritage—both sets of her grandparents were British—this was like opening an old and familiar storybook. One after another, the names she knew came into view. Big Ben…Westminster Abbey…Buckingham Palace…Trafalgar Square and Nelson's Column…Hyde Park…the Tower of London… Tessa gazed around her with absolute delight, and Charlie watched her with an enjoyment as intense as hers.

'Tomorrow I'll show you squirrels,' he said as the bus returned to their starting point. 'I'll just bet you've never seen a squirrel and I'll also bet you'll like them. We'll go to St James's Park. You can feed them there. They're as tame as be damned.'

Tessa came reluctantly back down to earth.

'Charlie, I can't,' she said. 'I have to go to Newcastle tomorrow.'

'I have plans about Newcastle.'

'What plans?'

'I need to go north myself. I'll drive you.'

Tess took a deep breath. This had to end, this fairytale time out.

'Charlie, I don't want you to drive me.'

'That seems ungracious,' Charlie said softly. 'Any particular reason? Don't you trust my driving?'

'I trust your driving but I don't trust you,' she confessed. 'You make me feel…'

'How do I make you feel, Tess?'

Silence.

The question was unanswerable. They stood in the busy street where they'd alighted from the bus, and Tess looked up at Charlie and everything she could think of to say was useless.

'Leave it,' she managed finally and turned away. 'Please...'

She walked twenty paces or so before Charlie followed her. He caught up with her at the corner, took her arm and made her pause.

'Okay,' he said softly. 'If you won't let me show you the squirrels tomorrow, come and see them now.'

'Now!' Tess glanced at her watch, startled. 'It's six o'clock...'

'It doesn't get dark over here like it does at home,' Charlie told her. 'This time of year it's light until ten. Come on. We're just by St James's Park. Ten minutes' walk won't hurt you. You've been sitting for hours.'

And once again, he brooked no opposition. Tessa either had to fight the hand that was pulling her inexorably forward—or go with him to inspect his dratted squirrels.

She was very glad she did.

The squirrels ranked with the most exquisite creatures she'd ever seen. Much smaller than she imagined and coloured russety grey, their bright little eyes were a welcome to London all on their own, and the way their tails bobbed and swayed as they leaped lightly over the lawns made her laugh.

She watched silently by Charlie's side, entranced.

St James's Park was wonderful—and so English! There was a very serious Englishman, complete in business suit, hat and waders, standing up to his thighs in the lake and feeding ducks with the intense concentration Tess would normally associate with something like dealings on the stock-market. There were nannies in neat uniforms with their little charges. There were tourists taking photographs. There was a spaniel chasing a ball.

She gazed around in delight, and almost forgot that Charlie's hand was holding hers. Almost, but not quite. Not quite at all.

'Okay. I guess it's time to go,' Charlie said at last, his voice faintly regretful. 'The problem with having a late breakfast instead of lunch is that by seven at night you're hungry as all get out. I'm starving. Come and find something to eat.'

'Okay.' Tess turned from the squirrel she'd been watching and smiled. Her hand was still loosely linked in Charlie's and she made no attempt to pull it away. 'Charlie, in case...in case there's no time to tell you properly in the morning... I mean...I just want to thank you. For this.'

She waved her spare hand toward the squirrels. 'For doing this for me. Not just rescuing me from Backblow Street and facing lawyers on my behalf. And for being nice when I slugged you and for showing me my squirrels. But for just being here for me.' She sighed. 'I hope you find a very nice wife, Charlie Cameron. One who'll love you and save your castle and make you very, very happy.'

Charles looked down at her, his dark eyes fathomless.

The early evening sun cast soft shadows over the couple standing on the lawn. At their feet, a pair of squirrels were arguing over what was left of one of last autumn's acorns.

'I have news for you, Tess Flanagan,' Charlie said softly. 'I already have.'

And, before she could guess what he intended, he bent his head and kissed her.

Tess froze. She froze for two whole seconds as his mouth met hers. And then his arms pulled her tight against him, and somehow...somehow she had to respond.

She had to push him away.

She could do no such thing. Somehow her arms and her brain were no longer connected. Her brain said get this man away, but her arms wouldn't work. An electrical fault somewhere...

That was just what it felt like. An electrical short circuit. Like something had fused—was fusing. Was going up in flames!

Tess gave a tiny moan and tried again but the same thing happened. And then she forgot about her arms. She forgot about everything. There was just Charlie, his body against hers, his mouth, his hands...Charlie holding her and making everything else disappear.

He pulled her closer and Tess tried not to let herself fall against him, but there was gravity or magnetism or something so darned strong it was irresistible working against her. Or working for her. Reeling her in.

Her breasts were on fire where they pressed against Charlie's chest and there was a fire starting below...a fire that was moving upward until her head seemed like it'd explode from heat.

And Charlie's tongue found its way into her mouth, tasting her, and Tessa's knees suddenly didn't work any more. It didn't matter. She was holding him and he was holding her and all there was in her world was Charlie.

Dear God... Dear God!

Somehow sanity got a look-in. A glimpse. A sliver of thought process broke through and she managed to haul herself half an inch back from his mouth.

'No...'

'You don't mean that.'

'Charlie!'

That reached him. The shock in her tone broke

through the heat haze and Charlie let her go. She stepped back, and stepped back further.

At their feet the squirrels gazed up with bemused curiosity.

Did the squirrels look at humans with the same interest as humans looked at squirrels? Tessa thought irrelevantly. What did they think of her conduct here? And she almost laughed. Good grief. She was close to hysteria. What on earth was she doing?

Charlie was standing looking down at her, his gentle eyes searching, waiting for her to come back to him. Waiting for her to say she'd marry him?

This was crazy. Crazy! The man was seducing her for a castle, for heaven's sake, and she had her whole life to plan and castles didn't come into it anywhere. Ben...Donald...Australia.

'We're nuts,' she said faintly.

'Nope.' He grinned, that damned infuriating grin that had her heart doing handstands. 'The squirrels would be more interested if we were nuts. Come here.'

'Why?' She glared.

'I want to kiss you again.'

'Well, I don't want to kiss you.' For goodness' sake, why was her heart racing like a silly schoolgirl's?

'Yes, you do. I could feel it. Do you kiss Donald like that?'

'I didn't kiss you,' she snapped.

'Yes, you did,' he said mildly. 'And very nice it was too.'

'I did not!'

He held up his hands in a placating gesture, and—drat him—he was laughing again. 'Okay, lady. I kissed you and you fought and screamed and protected your virtue like anything. I'm lucky you didn't go into full attack mode again. What will we do for dinner?'

'I should go back to Primrose Place,' she said darkly, glaring. Her world was spinning dangerously out of control here. Tessa's feet still felt as if they weren't quite on the ground.

'What, back to Backblow Street?' Charlie demanded, startled. 'Was my kiss that bad?'

'Yes. No. I don't know.'

'You did enjoy the kiss,' Charlie said in smug voice. 'It's got you all in a twitter.' He took two steps toward her and tucked her arm possessively into his arm. Entwined her fingers with his fingers. 'Do you know you look beautiful when you're twittered?'

Tess hauled back, but the hand held.

'I am not...'

'Not what?' he asked benevolently and Tessa glared.

'I am not twittered, Charlie Cameron,' she managed. 'I am angry. Of all the overbearing, arrogant...'

'We earls are like that. I told you. It's in our job description.'

'To think you can ride roughshod over what I want...'

'We've been doing it for generations.'

'I did not want to kiss you.'

'You did so.' He patted her hand with avuncular good nature. 'Now just hush, there's a good girl, and let me think where to take you to dinner. What do you want to eat?'

'I don't want to eat anything!'

'Yes, you do. I don't want an anorexic bride.' He smiled, a lazy, infuriating, charming smile that made her quite simply want to box his ears. Or kiss him again.

Box his ears. She needed to box his ears! But she'd already hurt him and the bruise on the side of his face made her want to... Want to what? Surely she wasn't thinking what she thought she was thinking?

Luckily, Charlie was concentrating on his stomach.

'We need a pub,' he was saying sagely. 'And I know just the pub. The Dog and Thistle on the Thames. They have quite simply the best roast beef and Yorkshire pudding of any pub in England. Followed by spotted dick and all washed down with warm beer.'

'I feel sick,' Tessa said faintly.

'I can see you do.' Charlie appeared to consider. 'All right,' he said in the voice of a man granting a very large concession. 'We'll let the English keep their warm beer and we'll stick to cold ale. The Dog and Thistle have ice-cold Fosters on tap for any wandering Australians such as you, my sweet. We'll feed you roast beef and Yorkshire pudding and spotted dick, our Tess, but we'll let you acclimatize gradually to warm beer. Now...any objections?'

Tess could think of a hundred objections. A million. For now though... For now there was only the feel of Charlie's hand in hers, the twinkle in his dark eyes and the knowledge that her alternative was dreary lodgings in Primrose Place.

She should head straight for Primrose Place.

It's only for one night, she told herself carefully. Tomorrow you never have to see this man again. What harm can one night do?

She knew exactly what harm one night could do. She looked up at Charlie Cameron and felt her knees quiver all over again. Primrose Place in Backblow Street was the sensible alternative.

But Charlie was at her side. Charlie Cameron, Earl of Dalston. Charlie for one night.

'Bring on your Yorkshire pudding then,' she said faintly. 'But just remember, Charlie Cameron. I'm an engaged lady, and I have some morals.

'Of course you do,' Charlie said softly. 'Your morals stick out a mile. They have from the moment I first set eyes on you. That's exactly the reason I intend to marry you.'

Tessa woke the next morning to a state of well-being she hadn't known for years. She lay cocooned in her wonderful bed, the morning sun streaming in her window and she thought for a minute she must be dreaming.

The Earl of Dalston was singing in the shower.

Her lips twitched at the sound. Charlie had a rich, baritone voice and it was resounding along the hall and through the walls as he sang in a broad Scottish accent. What was he singing?

'Will ye gang to the Hie-lans, Tessa Flanagan?

'My bride and my darling to be?'

Good grief!

Tessa hauled her pillows over her face, but her lips twitched. You had to give the man marks for trying.

Somewhat to her surprise, he'd left her to go to bed early last night. They'd had a lovely dinner and had walked home through the streets of Belgravia at about nine, but then he'd excused himself and had locked himself in his study. She'd heard the murmur of his voice on the telephone as she'd gone to bed and she'd wondered at the sound. His voice had seemed clipped and urgent, the traces of lazy laughter completely gone.

There was a Charles Cameron she hadn't met yet, she thought. Charles Cameron, businessman.

That he had to be a businessman she was sure. Any large-scale farmer in Australia—any farmer who could afford a light plane to fly to Melbourne once a month—couldn't be stupid, and there'd been nothing stupid in the way Charlie had squared off with the lawyer yesterday. He was sharp as nails.

What would he be like as a husband? Stupid thought. *Stupid thought!* So why did she keep thinking it?

She'd gone to bed but sleep hadn't come. It had almost been unexpected—that he'd brought her home and then calmly said goodnight and left her.

It's what you wanted, isn't it? she demanded of herself. Yeah, well…

What would he be like as a lover?

'Well, you'll never know, Tess girl,' she muttered to herself, hauling herself out of bed with a sigh and heading for the shower. 'Because you're engaged to be married to Donald, and today you're leaving Charlie Cameron for ever.'

Tessa might be leaving, but so was Charlie.

Tessa had finished breakfast and was on her second cup of tea and talking to Mary when Charlie appeared. The bruising on his eye had faded, Tess saw with relief. She'd been afraid by this morning he'd have a real black eye.

'I still need sympathy,' Charlie told her, seeing where she was looking. 'You want to check out what else you've done?' Then, grinning like a Cheshire cat at Tessa's blush, he took in Tessa's soft blue jeans and white blouse. And approved.

'Hey, Tess, I loved you in your jogging suit and I loved you in your business clothes, but I love you best of all in jeans.' But then he hesitated and his eyes turned wickedly thoughtful. 'I don't know, though. The bathrobe was pretty neat.'

Tessa's blush deepened to crimson.

'You behave yourself, Mr Charlie,' Mary said roundly. And then she paused. 'I mean—my lord.'

Charlie's smile faded. 'I like Charlie better,' he told Mary. 'I think we can do without the "my lord's".' Charlie parked his backside on the kitchen table and took a slice of toast from the pile. 'Honestly, Mary, why make all this? You know I've already eaten and I refuse to let you fatten our Tessa.'

'She could do with fattening.'

'Nope.' Charlie's eyes crinkled as he looked again at Tessa. 'She's just perfect. Tess, can you be ready to go in thirty minutes?'

'Go?' Tessa said blankly.

'Go.' Charlie looked at his watch. 'We leave for Newcastle at nine. I need to see a man about a dog in Leeds at one and then I thought we could go straight through.'

'But I'm catching a train,' Tessa told him, her face set. There was no way this man could bulldoze her. 'I checked the timetable when I arrived at the coach station. There's a train at ten.'

'Maybe there is. My car's more comfortable.'

'I prefer to catch the train.'

'No, you don't. You're just saying that because you don't want to put me to inconvenience. Or you don't trust me. Which is it?'

And Mary and Charlie both looked at her with interest.

Tessa flushed. 'I'm sure you don't need to go anywhere near Newcastle,' she managed, and Charlie smiled.

'So it's the "I don't want to be a bother" reason. That's great. I'd hate to think you don't trust me. Mary, tell Tess where I have to go.'

'I gather you need to go to the castle?' Mary asked, and Charles nodded. Was Tess imagining it, or did the smile slip a bit at the word 'castle'.

'You know I do.'

'Then Newcastle-upon-Tyne's hardly out of his way at all.' Mary beamed. 'I'll tell Henry to stow your luggage in the car, dear,' she told Tessa. 'You will bring

Tess back for a nice long visit, though, my lord, now won't you?'

'Mary, I can't.' Tessa's voice was practically a wail. 'Look, I'd love to come back here, but I need to see my nephew and sort out a few things and get back to Australia.' She took a deep breath. 'For a start, I'm only on two weeks' leave.'

'You're a working girl?' Charlie asked with interest. 'What do you do?'

Tess sighed. She just knew he was changing the subject here, and she shouldn't be deflected. 'I'm a nursing sister at Yaldara Bay Hospital.'

'A nurse.' Charlie's cat-got-the-cream look deepened. 'Hey, I'll just bet you look great in a uniform. Uniforms do all sorts of funny things to me. I've even been known to get excited when Mary puts on her apron. Henry has to tip buckets of cold water over me. And a whole nurse's uniform...'

'You get out of here, Mr Charlie,' Mary told him, chuckling. 'Don't you go listening to his nonsense, Miss Tess. But a nurse...' She gave a satisfied little smile. 'Well and well and well. That'll do very nicely. Now don't you go making any more fuss about trains. You let his lordship take you wherever you want to go.'

'You heard the lady,' Charlie said smugly. 'Go on, Tess. Just let his lordship take you wherever you want to go.'

Good grief!

By the time they arrived in Newcastle it was four thirty and Charlie Cameron knew just about all there was to know about Tessa. He'd asked question after question and she'd answered them.

In contrast, she'd asked questions of Charlie and he'd changed the subject.

Tess found herself more and more intrigued. On one level, Charlie Cameron could be taken as a rich and good-for-nothing playboy. Sitting at the wheel of his expensive Jaguar—they'd left Henry in London—dressed now in tailored trousers and linen shirt, he looked every inch a man of idle and expensive habits.

Until you looked at his hands. Charlie Cameron's hands were worn and calloused from sheer hard work, and his face was weathered and lined from the sun. He worked his land, Tess could see. No matter how much money this man possessed, he worked side by side with his men.

And the man joked all the time—but underneath the joking there was steel.

Why was he helping her? Tess wondered. Did he really believe he could persuade her to marry him? Did he really want to? It didn't make any sense at all.

Meanwhile, she sat back in the luxury of his expensive car and tried to concentrate on the views. After all, this was her first trip to England, she told herself. She should be soaking in the history of the place—the quaint stone walls—thatched roofs—hedgerows—lambs with black faces...

Instead, all she saw was Charlie.

They stopped briefly in Leeds, where Charlie left her to her own devices while he 'saw a man about a dog'. Tess wrote a perfunctory postcard to Donald and another to the hospital staff back home, but Charlie's business took him only half an hour. They ate at a pub—'the best food in England is found in pubs' Charlie told her—and were on their way again.

Tess found herself wondering just what Charlie's business had been. Whatever it was, it made the strained look she was beginning to detect behind his eyes even more obvious.

He wasn't telling her. She might tell him her worries, but Charles Cameron kept his to himself.

Some two hours later they pulled up outside a solid, Edwardian terrace in one of Newcastle's most prosperous streets. Home of Mrs Blainey. And Ben. Tessa's nephew. Tessa looked up at its imposing façade and felt pretty much the same as she had outside the lawyers. Intimidated.

Still, she had a weapon now. She fingered the copy of Christine's will in her pocket. Mrs Blainey had no choice but to let her see Ben. Tess was his guardian.

She swung her legs out of the car and then Charlie was at the passenger side helping her out.

'I... Thank you,' she said dubiously. 'I should say goodbye now.'

'But you don't want to?' he said hopefully and Tessa looked up into his labrador-puppy-hopeful expression and burst out laughing.

'You never give up, do you?'

'Nope.' He grinned. 'Come on. Let me meet the dragon.'

'She might not be a dragon,' Tessa said. 'Look, she loves Ben and she wants to keep him. That's not a crime.'

'Not wanting you to see Ben is.'

'She's right in that it might upset him.'

'Whose side are you on?' Charlie said in frustration. 'I'm on your side, but you're vacillating. Come on, Tess, lass. You're not wearing pantyhose today. Gird those loins of yours and let's get this over with.'

'Charlie...'

'You don't mean to tell me you've come all the way around the world and you're going to change your mind about seeing him now?'

'But what if I do upset him?'

'Tessa!' Charlie's tone was exasperated. Before she could stop him, he took both her hands in his and held them fast. 'Tessa, you're Ben's family. As far as I know, Ben has a grandmother and an aunty and that's *it*. If you and Mrs Blainey decide he shouldn't have an aunty because it might remind him of his mother—well, that's ridiculous. It means he's lost half the family he has left. He hasn't completely lost his mother when he has you. If you bail out now, then he's lost his last link.'

'But...'

'Tessa, your heart told you Mrs Blainey was wrong when she didn't want you to come here,' Charlie said softly. The grip of his hands tightened. 'Follow your heart, Tess. Nothing else. Just follow your heart.'

He looked down at her for a long, long moment—and then walked forward and rang the bell.

Tess stared. There was something twisting inside her that she'd never felt before. Something that had stirred for the first time yesterday—standing in the sunlight with this man holding her—kissing her. She hadn't recognized it fully then, but it jabbed like a knife now, rocking her foundations. Making her stare at Charlie as if she'd never seen him before.

She didn't have time to examine the sensation more. The door swung open. A maid stood in the doorway—fifty-something, starched and uniformed and with a face like a brick.

'Yes?' she said in a voice that dripped icicles.

'We're here to see Mrs Blainey,' Charlie said cheerfully. He reached back and took Tessa's hand in his, urging her forward. 'Is she home?'

'May I ask who's calling?' The woman's eyes drifted to the Jaguar parked behind them, and the ice melted just a touch.

'I'm Miss Tessa Flanagan from Australia,' Tess told her. 'Ben's aunty.'

The face froze again and the door started to close.

'I'm sorry. Mrs Blainey isn't...'

Charlie's foot moved forward, blocking the closing of the door.

'Mrs Blainey isn't in?' he asked. 'There's someone upstairs. I saw her face at the window just now and I'm betting it's your mistress. Go and tell her we're here, there's a good girl.'

The woman gasped. 'Kindly remove your foot from the door.'

'You'll just shut it if I do,' Charlie pointed out. 'And I know you don't want to do that. We'll just wait in the hall until Mrs Blainey comes down.'

'She doesn't want to see you,' the woman said.

'Very well.' The steel flooded straight back into Charlie's voice. He didn't look at Tess. His gaze locked on the maid, and Tess thought if she was the maid, she'd quail before it. 'If Mrs Blainey doesn't wish to see us, then we'll do without. Could you pack Master Ben's belongings and bring the little boy down here, please?' Charlie glanced at his watch. 'We need to be gone in thirty minutes.'

'What do you mean—pack Master Ben's belongings?' the woman gasped.

'Tessa is Master Ben's legal guardian,' Charlie said, and his voice was ruthless. 'If Tess can't satisfy herself that Master Ben is being well cared for—and she needs to speak to Mrs Blainey to do that—then she has no choice but to take him with her. *Now.* Could you tell Mrs Blainey that, please?' He smiled his blandest smile, and the sharp intelligence behind his eyes was obvious to them all. 'We're waiting.'

They didn't have to wait long. Charlie's words acted

like a starter's gun. They were ushered into a formal sitting room and, within thirty seconds, Mrs Blainey sailed into view.

There was no other way of describing it. Margot Blainey was a woman accustomed to power, and it showed in every inch of her bearing. Tall and slim, dressed in severest black with her pure white hair drawn tightly into an elegant chignon that no stray wisp would dare escape from, Margot Blainey exuded authority from every pore.

She stepped two feet into the room and stared straight at Tessa. And gasped.

'Oh, no,' she said faintly. The aura of battleship faded and she stepped backward. She produced a wisp of dainty linen and drew it to her eyes, visibly upset. 'I knew it would be like this,' she whispered. 'You're so like darling Christine...'

Tessa frowned. She'd never had the impression that Christine and her mother-in-law were close. The opposite in fact. In her scant letters Christine had complained about her mother-in-law's overbearing nature from day one of her marriage. There was no denying that the woman was upset, though, and here was a solid reason to explain Tessa's frigid welcome.

'I'm sorry,' Tess said gently. 'I know how like Christine I am. I understand it's upsetting, but I had to come. I had to see Ben.'

The woman didn't emerge from her handkerchief. 'Ben will break his heart when he sees you.'

'Where is he?' Charlie asked. There was little gentleness in his tone and the woman lowered her handkerchief to give him a glacial stare.

'He's upstairs in the nursery. I can't permit you to see him. It's too soon...'

'You'd like him to forget his mother before he sees Tessa?'

'I didn't say that.' If they'd really existed behind the handkerchief, the woman's tears had vanished as quickly as they'd come. 'It's just too soon.'

'I'd still like to see him,' Tessa said.

'You can't.'

Alone, the woman's denial might have stopped Tess, but Charlie was in battle on her behalf. 'Yes, she can,' he said bluntly. 'According to her sister's will, Tessa's his guardian.'

Silence. The handkerchief disappeared entirely. Anger replaced the tears.

'I don't know where Miss Flanagan received that information...' Margot said finally.

'She read it,' Charlie told her. Tessa flashed a look at Charlie. He almost sounded as if he was enjoying himself. 'I did too,' he continued. 'The nice lawyer at Scott, Scott and McPherson gave us a copy.'

'But I told them...'

'You told them to delay showing it Tessa,' Charlie said thoughtfully. 'Maybe until she got back to Australia? That wasn't exactly thoughtful, now was it?'

There was no trace of sadness on Margot Blainey's face now. Her overriding emotion was just plain fury. 'Look, I don't know who you are...'

'I'm acting on behalf of Tessa here,' Charlie said cheerfully. He placed a hand on Tessa's shoulder. 'We need to see Ben.'

'I don't think...'

'You have no choice,' Charlie told her. 'Please go and fetch him.'

Mrs Blainey glared for one long minute. Charlie stared blandly back. Impasse. Steel meeting steel. And there was no doubting the outcome. Mrs Blainey had met her match.

Finally the woman rang a bell on the table. The sour-faced maid appeared as if she'd been waiting on the other side of the door.

'Tell Emma to bring the child down,' the woman said dourly. She glared from Tess to Charlie and back again. 'But don't blame me if no good comes of this.'

As far as Tess could see, Ben wasn't upset to see her. He wasn't even particularly interested.

The child was towed into the room by a nanny who looked little more than a child herself. He stood tucked behind his nanny's skirt, his thumb firmly wedged into his mouth and an expression on his face of blank compliance.

'Ben...'

The child looked the same as he had in his photographs. He was a tiny waif of a child, with fair, curly hair, big brown eyes and a little too thin for his years. He was wearing matching tartan overalls, cap and boots, little Lord Fauntleroy-style. He looked hot.

Tess walked slowly forward and knelt down before him so her eyes were level with his. She took two limp little hands in hers.

'Ben, I'm your Aunty Tess. I'm your mummy's sister, all the way from Australia. Mummy must have told you about me.'

Nothing. Ben stared at her as if she might have come from Mars.

'Do you want me to stay, ma'am?' That was the nanny. The girl was wearing a nanny's uniform that was almost incongruous on one so young. She had one earring in one ear, three in the other and one in her nose.

'No, thank you, Emma.' Mrs Blainey sniffed. 'I'll call you when I wish you to take him upstairs again.'

'Just a moment.' Tess rose and stopped the girl with a hand on her arm. 'Your name's Emma, right?'

The girl gave her a long look of interest. 'Yeah. And you must be Christine's—Mrs Blainey junior's—sister. You do look like her.' She smiled, and for the first time Tess could see why she'd been hired. There was real friendliness in the smile. The girl touched Ben's fair hair. 'Eh, your Aunty Tess looks just like your mum, Ben. Isn't that neat?'

'Have you been looking after Ben for long?'

'A year,' Emma said diffidently. 'Maybe a bit more.'

'And will you stay on with him now?'

'Well…' The girl cast a doubtful look at Mrs Blainey. 'I dunno. My folks are from the Lake District. But if Ben's here and Mrs Blainey wants me to stay…' Once again, she touched Ben's curls. 'Ben and me are friends. I'd miss him.' She ruffled his hair. 'I'll be upstairs waiting for you, Ben boy. See you soon.' And she took herself off.

Ben reacted then. He grabbed at her skirt, but missed. The door closed behind Emma and Ben walked over and tried to open it to follow.

'Ben, stay where you are,' Margot Blainey ordered.

It was the voice of authority and Ben knew it. He stopped, turned around, and the mantle of submission fell again. A tear trickled silently down the little boy's cheek. Only one, before he swallowed and kept the rest at bay.

Tess took a step toward him—and the child flinched.

Silence.

The silence went on and on. Tess simply didn't know where to start. Dear God, he didn't know her… To push herself on him—to make those tears fall—was unbearable.

It was Charlie who finally broke the silence. Of course it was Charlie. He glanced from Tess to Mrs Blainey and back to Tess. Then he simply walked across and scooped the little boy into his arms.

'Hey, Ben, I'm Charlie,' he said, ignoring the little boy's instinctive arching of withdrawal. He walked over to the window and pulled back the heavy curtains. 'That's my car out there. It's a Jaguar. It's black. Is your car black?'

'Red,' the child whispered. 'Daddy's car's red.'

'What's your favourite colour?'

'Yellow.' The little boy wriggled in Charlie's arms until he could reach into his pocket. He hauled out a tiny model car—bright yellow. 'Emmy gave me a yellow car.'

'It's great.' Charles inspected it with all seriousness. 'It's a Volkswagen, Ben.'

'I know. Emmy showed me in a book.'

'Emmy's your friend?'

'Yes,' Ben said definitely. 'She said we had to come here so we did. I wanted to stay at home but Emmy brought me here in Grandma's car.'

The conversation between Charlie and Ben continued, but Mrs Blainey wasn't interested.

'Well? You've seen him,' she snapped to Tess. 'You're not seriously considering taking an active rôle in his guardianship? The child knows me. This is his country. It's his home.'

Tess nodded. It seemed unarguable. 'You definitely want to continue looking after him?'

'Of course I do,' the woman said. 'He's my grandson. He's British. His place is here.' She smiled. 'Between us, his nanny and I will see that he has everything that he needs. You can be quite sure of that.'

Silence. There seemed little else to say.

'I'll come and see him again before I go home,' Tess told her. 'If I may.'

'If you must,' the woman said, and her voice was repelling. 'Though, as I've said, I believe Ben has enough adjusting to do already without being exposed to any more unsettling influences.' She walked to the door. 'Now, if you'll excuse me, I really am very busy.'

CHAPTER FIVE

THEY left Ben with his grandmother.

'I can't take him away,' Tessa said, as the door closed behind them. 'She loves him.'

'Emma loves him,' Charlie said. 'I doubt *that* woman loves anyone.'

'Then why does she want to keep him?'

'Because she's a control freak. If there's something to control, that woman will want to control it.'

'You're being unfair.'

'Is that because you don't want Ben yourself?'

'I *do* want him. If I thought Ben needed me...'

'He does need you.'

'No, he doesn't. He's got Emma...'

'Emma's a paid employee, Tess,' Charlie said bluntly. 'She's about seventeen, if that. Give her another twelve months and she'll fall madly in love. Maybe sooner. She'll leave to raise her own family and Ben will be on his own again.'

'Are you saying I should take Ben out of there now?' Tess demanded, her colour mounting. 'Take Ben away from the only people he knows?'

'I'm saying you should think about it.'

'I'm thinking.' Tess glared. 'Now...if you don't mind... This is definitely time to say goodbye.'

'Where are you going?'

'To the Lake District,' Tessa told him. 'To Borrowdale. Mr Scott gave me the keys to Christine's house. I need to figure what to do with all her...with

Ben's things. I guess I'll set the house up as a rental property until Ben comes of age.'

'I'll take you there.'

'No.'

'Don't be bloody stupid, Tess,' Charlie said, exasperated. 'Don't look a gift horse in the mouth. Just get in the car and shut up.'

Tess looked at him sideways, and frowned. 'That sounds like you're angry.'

'I have cause to be angry. You're being blind.'

'Then if you're angry—if you disapprove of my decision— then maybe you'd best leave me alone.' Tess took a deep breath, mentally girding her pantyhose. 'I don't need your approval, Charles Cameron. I can manage on my own.'

'That might be true,' Charlie told her, his anger disappearing as fleetingly as it had arrived. 'But it's time to pay back debts.'

'Debts?'

'Debts.' He smiled then, disapproval giving way to his constantly lurking laughter. 'I've given you a night's accommodation, lady. Now, I need somewhere to sleep. Tonight we'll kip at your sister's house in the Lake District. And tomorrow, I'll show you my castle.'

'I don't...'

'You don't want to give me accommodation?'

'Charlie, I don't know if I can,' Tess said doubtfully. 'I've never been to Christine's house. All I have is an address.'

'Yeah, well, my address up here is Castlerigg, north of Keswick and almost on the Scottish border,' Charlie told her. 'There's a caretaker's residence but the caretaker is about eighty and has kittens if she has to make up a spare bed. She needs a month's notice in writing or she threatens me with angina or stroke or at the very least a spot of death.'

'But the castle...'

'In the castle I have battlements, towers, a dungeon, the remains of a moat, but no roof and certainly no beds. Also brambles and poison ivy and all sorts of nasties. Castlerigg was last inhabited three hundred years ago. Your sister's house has been empty for a week and it's within an hour's driving of Castlerigg.'

'But...'

Charlie's voice turned suddenly sympathetic. 'Tess, I know what you're going through here. Your sister's dead and her house will be full of ghosts.' Drat the man; he really could read her mind. Charlie's smile was gentle and understanding. A smile that suddenly came close to making her want to weep. He touched her face with his fingers and the sensation burned.

'But your ghosts are known, Tess,' he continued. 'And I'd imagine they wish you well. Mine, on the other hand, are probably clanking round in full suits of armour and I'm not sure what they wish me. I'm not the least sure they approve of what's in store for their castle. So...let's deal with your ghosts first and my ghosts in the morning.'

'Charlie...'

'Tess, I'm too tired to argue,' Charlie told her, and the look of strain flitted back behind his eyes, adding force to his words. 'Let's just do it.'

There was silence for the rest of the drive to Borrowdale, which was just as well. The strain showing in Charlie's eyes was nothing to the strain in his head. A pulse was pounding like a sledgehammer and he had the strongest urge just to point the car at the nearest motorway, head for the nearest airport and get himself back to Australia. Leave this mess for others to sort out.

How on earth could he hope to sort it on his own? he thought bitterly. And what the hell was he doing here? With this girl?

His half-joking suggestion was becoming more concrete by the moment. Marriage… As far as he could see, it was the only way out of disaster.

But…marriage to Tess?

Maybe he could use the little boy as a lever.

Charlie glanced sideways at Tessa's troubled face and felt a sharp stab of guilt. He couldn't do this. It was the lowest of the low.

But…what on earth else could he do?

The Borrowdale valley ran south from Keswick along the shores of Derwent Water, and there wasn't a lovelier part of the Lake District. Charlie pulled up before a two-storey home of soft grey stone. It looked old and gracious, its garden a jumble of wild-flowers and roses tumbling over the stone walls in pink profusion.

'This can't be right.' Tess gazed at the house, astounded. 'Are you sure we have the right address?'

'Greyrigg Rise,' Charlie said, and pointed to the sign. 'I know riggs are two a penny around here, but there'd hardly be two Greyriggs on the one road.'

'But Christine hated this place,' Tess said slowly. 'It's entailed or something so she and her husband couldn't sell, but they were desperate to move to London.'

'More fool them.' Charlie's mischief flashed out again. 'Hey, we could live here, Tess. Me and you and Ben. It's a great family home.'

'Yeah?' Humour him, she told herself firmly. 'Well, that'd make the four of us.'

'Four?'

'You and Ben and me—and my Donald. With you

sleeping on the guest bed. So on your bike, Charles Cameron, or shut up and let's have a look at this place.'

The house was as lovely inside as it was out, Tess decided as they explored. Christine had always had an eye for colour, and her husband had had money.

But…it was like something…

'Something out of *Vogue*,' Tess said, frowning. She'd expected to be upset, going through Christine's home, but instead… Apart from two rooms upstairs used by Ben and his nanny, the house seemed as impersonal as a display home.

'It needs a couple of dogs, a few photos and some mucky wellingtons at the back door,' Charlie agreed. 'My wellies.'

'Charlie…'

He grinned and held up a placating hand. 'Okay. Okay. But there are no ghosts here, Tess.'

'I don't think Christine and John can have been here very often.'

'No. And that explains Ben's attitude to you.' Charlie crossed to the Aga and checked it. No one had turned the gas off. The range was still warm. 'Cup of tea?'

'Lovely. But…' Tess frowned. 'Ben's attitude?'

'He wasn't upset because you looked like his mother,' Charlie said gently. 'It's as if his mother was just one more person in his life.'

Tess turned this over. 'Christine and her husband were very social.'

'Mmm.'

'You can't criticize her.'

'Because she's dead? Of course I can,' Charlie told her bluntly. 'I can criticize anyone I like when I see what a mess that little boy's in.'

'He's not in a mess.'

'Yes, he is, Tess.' Charlie sighed. He stared sightlessly at the kettle for a long minute—and then seemed to make up his mind. He left the stove and strode over to grip her shoulders, ignoring her instinctive recoil.

'Tess, Ben's stuck in a mausoleum of a house with a battleaxe as a grandmother and the only person who loves him—or even likes him—is a kid not much older than he is. His grandmother's as warm as a slab of cold cement. Like it or not, if you care about him you're going to have to do some loving yourself.'

'I'll phone Donald tonight,' Tess said stiffly, trying to ignore the feel of his hands. The strength and warmth... 'I'll see what he says.'

'You'll tell him you're taking Ben home with you?'

'I don't know.' With an effort, Tess shook his hands away from her, took a step back and glared. 'Charlie, Ben's happy with Emma. You can see she's fond of him. I can't tear him away.'

Charlie folded his arms and surveyed her thoughtfully. And shook his head. 'Tess, he'll be happier long term if he can find someone to be a mother to him. Emma's not that.'

'Neither am I.'

'Because you don't want to be?' Charlie's voice gentled. 'Or is it...is it that your dreadful Donald won't be his father?'

He was so close to the mark that she gasped. 'This...this is none of your business,' she managed.

'If you don't want to stay here, then Ben could share our castle,' Charlie told her. 'There's room to spare for one small boy. And what small boy doesn't like castles?'

'Oh, for heaven's sake... I thought you said your castle doesn't have a roof,' Tess said, exasperated. 'Charlie, what I do about Ben doesn't concern you. I don't know what I'll do about Ben, but I am *not* rushing into anything.'

'Sometimes you have to rush,' Charlie said gently. 'Life's short, Tess. Ben's three years old and no one loves him. If you take a year to make up your mind, the damage could be irreversible.'

'And the damage if I make the wrong decision?'

'What does your heart tell you to do?'

Tess closed her eyes. She knew exactly what her heart was telling her. It was screaming at her to rush back to Newcastle, gather that forlorn little boy in her arms and love him as her own.

But Donald didn't want him, and Donald had given her solid, sensible reasons why Ben should stay in England.

He was better off in his own country—with his grandmother. That was her head talking. Not her heart.

'Tell you what,' Charlie said softly, watching the conflicting emotions wash across her face. She was vacillating. If he moved fast, then, maybe... 'Why don't we leave this for a few hours? I want to show you something.'

'What?'

'There's no need to sound suspicious. It's a tourist attraction, and you're a tourist.'

'No, I'm not.'

'Well, pretend to be,' Charlie said in irritation. 'Tess, I want to show you this, and the way I'm feeling I'm likely to pick you up, hurl you over my shoulder and cart you there by force. It's just on seven now. We'll find something to eat in Keswick and go from there. We'll be home here by dark.'

'Promise?' Tess said and there was no mistaking the suspicion in her voice.

'I promise.'

'Well...' Tess hesitated. If Charlie was definitely staying...

'Well, what?'

'If you want to be useful…' There were so many emotions charging around her head she didn't know where to start, but she'd come to England with two strong intentions and Charlie mustn't deflect her. Seeing Ben had been one. The other…

'Charlie, my sister and her husband were buried here last week. I need…'

She didn't have to finish. 'You need to go to the graveyard and you'd like some company,' Charlie said softly. 'I can do that. I told you, Tess. I'll face your ghosts with you.' He took her hand in his and held it hard. This could work. *It could!* 'And after that, we'll do the tourist bit. Together.'

Charlie took her to the cemetery and stood silently by while Tess said farewell to her twin.

In the end, it wasn't as bad as Tess had expected. It was as if she'd lost Christine years ago, when her twin had decided to abandon her family and come to England. Christine had lost interest in her Australian family, and the desolation Tess felt was more for a separation that was years old than a recent death.

All the same, she was glad Charlie was with her. He stood a couple of paces apart, sensing her need for solitude, but his presence was a warm and comforting affirmation that she wasn't alone in the world.

She shouldn't feel alone, she told herself. She had Donald… Donald. Donald was starting to seem more and more a vague and distant shadow. She turned from the graveside, Charlie took her arm and Donald slipped still further into shadowland.

After that, Charlie took her into Keswick and introduced her to chip butties.

'You have to be kidding,' Tess said faintly, looking at her greasy concoction with amazement. 'Chips in bread! What nation can possibly serve chips in bread and expect paying customers to eat it?'

'Try it.' Charlie grinned. 'I know it's everything that's bad for you, but Henry introduced me to chip butties when I was eight years old and it was love at first bite. My first love.' He sighed nostalgically. 'You're my second.'

Tessa flushed. 'Charlie...'

'Shut up, there's a love,' Charlie told her firmly. 'And wrap yourself around the best cuisine Britain has to offer.'

Chip butties demolished, Charlie took her to Castlerigg.

Tess saw the sign a mile out of Keswick and frowned. 'Castlerigg... Isn't that the name of your castle?'

'Yep,' Charlie told her. 'Maybe it's coincidence—but maybe not. My guess is my ancestors felt about this place the way I do. Identical names for two of my favourite places.'

'So is this place a castle?'

'No, again. Wait and see.'

It wasn't a castle. It was a circle of stones.

Put like that—a simple group of stones—it didn't sound much at all, but the sight that met Tessa when Charlie parked his car and they climbed over the stile to see what lay beyond the wall just took her breath away.

Castlerigg Stone Circle.

'The locals refer to it as a Druids' circle,' Charlie told her, noting her look of awe with quiet satisfaction. 'But it's older than the Druids. Four thousand years old. Or more. Older than time itself.'

Time is... Time will be... Time here was nothing. Time stood still.

The circle was simplicity itself. Fifty or so boulders, mostly no taller than a man and many smaller, standing as stern sentinels on the brow of the hill. But where they were placed…

Standing in the centre of the circle, there were mountains all around them. Under their feet was lush pasture, filled with meadowsweet and buttercups. And when they raised their eyes there was only the mountains.

The sun was sinking and a faint hint of flame coloured the evening sky. Tessa felt all sorts of things stir within her as she gazed around. Up here, alone with Charlie—alone with the mountains and the stones that had been put here thousands of years before… Dear God…

Below the ridge, there were black-faced sheep placidly grazing as they'd been grazing here for generations. They paid Tess and Charlie no heed at all.

Tess might be living two thousand years ago. Four thousand. Or two thousand years in the future. There was nothing here but this simple, eloquent grandeur. A man and a woman, standing within a circle of stones.

A man and a woman…

Tess turned to Charlie and found him watching her from twenty feet away; watching her as a man might well have looked at a woman four thousand years before. There was a look in his eyes Tess knew. He wanted her. He wanted her as much as she wanted him.

Dear heaven, what was she thinking? She didn't want Charlie. She didn't!

He wanted her.

'Tess, the thing I want most in the world,' Charlie said conversationally, 'is to marry you. Up here, these stones are saying that life's fleeting. Take the joy where it offers, Tessa love, because it doesn't offer for long.' Charlie didn't move to touch her. He didn't need to. From twenty feet away, his eyes were a caress all by themselves.

There was total silence. The last rays of the sun fell

softly on Tessa's face while Charlie Cameron made love to her with his eyes. He made no move to touch her. He simply loved her.

'Why are you marrying Donald?' he asked, and the mountains waited for an answer.

Good grief... She should ignore the question. She should tell him once again to mind his own business. But, standing within the circle of ancient stones, it seemed there was nothing but the truth. Druids' circle or not, there was magic in this place. The mountains were asking the question, as well as Charlie, and she had to find an answer.

'Charlie, Donald's my friend,' she managed. 'He's been my friend since childhood.'

'I have friends,' Charlie said softly. Still he didn't move. The distance between them was a strange, unreal barrier, no way lessening the intimacy. 'I don't want to marry them, but they're still my friends.'

'Donald wants to marry me.'

Charlie shrugged. 'Well, then. So do I. But Tessa, I don't want to be your friend. I want to be your lover.' And his voice grew dreamy. 'Tess, does Donald want you like I want you? Does he...?'

'I don't...'

But he was brooking no interruptions. 'Tess, I want to take you to me...to remove every stitch of your clothing, piece after piece and see you as you really are. I want to see your beautiful self. I want to let my hands move over your soft skin. I want to feel the moistness of your lips and let my fingers drift from your face, down to your breasts...Tess, I'll bet you have the most beautiful breasts...'

What was he doing? He was making love to her with his words! From twenty feet away...

Tess stared across the circle at her man. Her man?

Yes. For this moment, this was what Charlie was. For this moment there was only Charlie in the world. Only his deep, caressing voice...

Tess couldn't move if she'd wanted to. Her knees were turning to jelly under her and somewhere a fire was building.

'I want to...'

'Charlie, don't...' She couldn't get her voice above a whisper and it died away to nothing.

'I want to find your thighs, Tessa. I can tell from here... You're every inch a woman and your thighs will be as a woman's should be. Soft, yielding, and yet eager. You want me as much as I want you, Tessa Flanagan, and it's my guess you're wanting me now... Aching for me... I'm a man and you're a woman and we're made for each other. I knew that the moment I saw you and if you don't know it yet, then you surely will. I want to take you to me as men have taken their women since the beginning of time. Take you and join you to me. And me to you. Two bodies. One heart.'

His voice faded to nothing. Unnoticed, the sun slipped further behind the mountains and the flaming glow started to disappear.

There was absolute silence. The mountains kept their counsel, watching with the patience of endless time.

'And afterwards,' Charlie said softly. 'Afterwards, Tess, I'd hold you in my arms, skin against skin, and I'd feel your heart beating against mine. With mine. One heartbeat, Tessa. Two bodies. One heart. For ever.'

Then he paused.

The moment broke.

For a second Tess thought he would come to her. And if he did... If he came, then she would have melted in his arms. There was no defence against what she was feeling right now. He could take her right now, on this sweet-smelling bed of pasture and if tourists came, then what the heck…

But Charlie's face had changed. Twisted. The shadows flickered down and, unnoticed, the sun disappeared completely behind the furthermost peak and the shadows closed…

Charlie shut his eyes in pain. 'Think about it, Tess,' he said roughly. Before she could gather her wits to say a word, he strode out of the circle, and Tessa was left standing staring after him, wondering what on earth had just happened.

They drove back to Borrowdale without speaking.

Tessa couldn't. She hardly looked at Charlie, just flicking him sidelong glances when she thought he wasn't watching.

Charles Cameron's face was set and grim. This was a different Charlie. A Charlie who'd laid his cards on the table and now expected to see hers?

But…something was wrong. Something Tess didn't understand. Why hadn't he come to her? Why hadn't he gathered her in his arms and claimed her as he'd said he wished—as he surely could, the way she was feeling? It was as if he were warring with himself and she didn't know why.

When they pulled up outside the house, Tess found she was shaking. Too much was happening, way too fast. Her foundations were shifting underneath her feet. She was half a world away from home, and everything she'd ever valued was being questioned.

Charlie was the first to break the silence.

'Hey, Tess, let's get this into perspective.' Charlie hauled her suitcase and his overnight bag into the living room. His voice was still grim, but he set their gear down and flicked a long finger over her cheek. A flick of friendship. A businesslike flick. 'Where will we sleep?'

Tess glanced up at him and then away.

'Did you know, you look as white as a ghost,' he told her, his voice gentling. He sighed. 'Tess, I don't ravish women against their will. We'll sleep separately until you say the word.'

Didn't ravish women against their will! What did he think he'd just done? And...what was he doing, saying they'd sleep separately? It was the last thing Tessa wanted.

'Why don't you sleep in Ben's bed upstairs?' Charlie said gently. 'There are no ghosts there.'

'And...and you?' Tess glanced toward her sister's bedroom. The door was open. The bed was huge—a king-sized bed with gorgeous white lace and frilly cushions.

'No,' Charlie told her, following her gaze. Once more he touched her face. 'That's a bit much. Even if the ghosts are friendly, that's a bit much.' And he leaned over and kissed her softly on the lips.

A feather kiss. A kiss of reassurance rather than passion. A kiss that sent a shudder through her entire body.

Where was the passion? her body screamed.

'Go and sleep,' Charlie said, and his hands held her away, at arm's length. 'But in your dreams, Tess... Know that life is transient and happiness is to be grasped with both hands, and held. Think about that, Tess. For me and for you, and for Ben. Think about that.'

But he didn't take her in his arms.

And when she woke in the morning, Charlie was gone.

CHAPTER SIX

TESS stood in her nightgown at the top of the stairs and gazed around with bewilderment.

Her body clock had had some adjusting to do, catching up to its broken sleep patterns of the last few days. She'd fallen into bed with the sound of Charlie making himself comfortable on the settee downstairs and, despite the turmoil in her heart, she had slept through until nine the next morning.

But now...

Charlie's overnight bag had disappeared. The bedclothes they'd found for the settee had been packed away.

Charlie...

The lurching of her stomach had nothing to do with the fact that she still thought Charles Cameron a sandwich short of a picnic. It had nothing to do with the fact that she was engaged to Donald, and Charles Cameron had no right to make a pass at her, much less propose marriage.

It had everything to do with the way Charlie looked at her. Donald never looked at her like that. Charlie Cameron made her feel every inch a woman.

Two bodies. One heart...

He'd gone.

Tess walked slowly down the stairs, making herself believe it had really happened.

Maybe he hadn't gone for good, her heart said. Maybe he'd just gone to buy a morning paper.

There was a note on the kitchen table and she grabbed it like a lifebuoy.

Tess. Decided in the night that it wasn't fair to drag you to the castle this morning. You need to come to terms with what's here but I'm needed there. Therefore I'm off and sooner gone, sooner back. Spend the next few of days thinking about me, Tessa love. You won't be out of my thoughts for a minute. Back on Saturday.

Tess bit her lip. Back on Saturday. Back in three long days. She could be gone by Saturday, she thought. Didn't Charlie realize?

Of course he didn't. Today was Wednesday. There was no way she could have the place ready for rental by Saturday. Charlie knew very well that she'd still be here.

She'd be here waiting for him.

No. Of course not. Ridiculous thought.

Okay. Tess glanced around the kitchen and squared her shoulders, trying to drive some sense into her stupid head, trying to see past the passion. Okay. Wherever Charlie had gone or what he was doing—or when he returned—didn't matter to her at all. There was work to be done, and the only way through it was through it.

Just put Charlie Cameron out of your head and get on with the rest of your life, she told herself harshly. Put Charlie Cameron right out of your head... How in heaven's name could she do that?

The lawyer in Penrith was a different sort of lawyer from the one Charlie had met with Tess. This man was older, greyer, and much, much more direct. He was being direct now.

'I don't see any way out of it, my lord.'

'Will you stop calling me "my lord",' Charlie said in weary exasperation. He raked his fingers through his hair and stared down at the papers. 'How the hell can my uncle have done this? What was in his mind?'

'To force you to marry,' the lawyer said dourly. He smiled a little sadly. 'Your uncle made the will after hearing gossip about you and some model or other. Don't think I didn't try to talk him out of it. So many lives...'

'It wasn't important to him that I marry,' Charlie said savagely. 'There's nothing to be gained by this. He's done it because he couldn't stand me.'

'He did try all means of blocking the entailment.' The lawyer sighed. 'I'm afraid I have to agree. Your uncle always was a difficult man and he didn't like you.'

Charlie closed his eyes and tried raking his hair again. It didn't help. 'So where does that leave me, Mr Roberts?'

'It's not really you that's...'

'It is,' Charlie said savagely. 'It's my inheritance and I'm responsible. What's the price to buy it back? Can I do it?'

The grim-faced lawyer looked across the desk at Charlie for a long, long moment. He liked this young man and he would have liked more than anything to give him some decent news. But there was none to give.

'There's an overseas consortium already interested,' he told him. 'They'll buy the lot.'

'For how much?'

The lawyer told him. Charlie blenched.

'That much?'

'At least. If not more.'

'Can I raise that?'

'Not with the stipulation about restoration. It simply isn't possible.' The lawyer leaned back in his chair and looked at him with sympathy. 'You could simply leave it. Walk away...'

'From my inheritance.'

'This isn't a wonderful inheritance as it stands.' The lawyer hesitated. 'But...is there no one?' He paused, edging around a subject he didn't like to raise. 'No girlfriend? Excuse me, my lord, but if ever you were thinking of marrying, then now's the time...'

'In *five weeks*?'

'Hasty marriages have been made before.'

Charles shook his head. 'I've been thinking about it,' he admitted. 'But...I can't put *this* pressure on a girl. Marry me or else...or else so much is lost.' He groaned. 'It's not fair.'

'The whole thing's not fair.' The lawyer gathered his papers together. 'In no way is it fair. But if there is a girl, my lord...' Then his voice softened as he looked at Charlie's haggard face. 'If there is a girl, then maybe now's the time... Maybe not to put financial pressure on, but have her marry you for yourself.' He allowed himself a wry little smile. 'You're not such a bad bargain, my lord. Swallow your scruples. It really would avert what seems to me to be irredeemable disaster.'

'Yeah?' Charlie glanced at the date on the calendar. 'Well, if I'm to marry an Australian girl... In Australia you need to give a month's notice before you can marry. That means if I want to marry...'

'Then you need to decide on a bride by next Friday,' the lawyer told him flatly, and allowed himself another grim smile. 'A week from today. And if I might say so, my lord, if anyone can do that, you can.'

Tessa stood outside, hanging sheets to dry and letting the morning sun shine on her face. Friday. Where was Charlie now?

It didn't matter.

It did.

She glanced down at her watch. Ten in the morning. Plus nine hours… If she rang Donald…

Why would she ring Donald? To tell him she was in love with another man?

Oh, for heaven's sake… She closed her eyes and shook her head. You're no such thing. Love! Just because he has sex appeal. You don't fall for sex appeal…

Yes, I do.

Then pack up and get out of here fast, Tessa Flanagan. Before you make the biggest mistake you could ever make in your life!

You can't leave.

Then grit your teeth and think of something other than Charlie.

Ha!

High on the battlements of Castlerigg—of his ancestral home—Charlie Cameron, thirteenth Earl of Dalston, stood looking over his terrain. His land. It stretched as far as the eye could see in whatever direction he looked.

It was beautiful country—wild and rugged and lovely. The fells and dales of Cumbria stretched all around him, reaching right up to the Scottish borders. You could almost see to Scotland from here.

But…the lawyer had said there was an overseas consortium already poised for the kill. What would they do with the place? Charlie thought bitterly, and he knew without having to answer.

Dear heaven…

Tessa. Tessa was his only solution. Would Tessa marry him?

The thought of Tessa Flanagan made him stir uneasily. She was the loveliest creature… If he hadn't met her now… Would he want to marry her, regardless?

He might not have thought of it, he decided honestly, turning his face into the warm south wind. His uncle was right when he'd assessed his nephew as not the type to marry. Women in general were far too desirable to Charlie Cameron for him to choose one in particular.

But, having now thought of Tessa as his wife, the possibility held distinct appeal. More than distinct appeal. The feel of Tess in his arms—her lips on his—had shaken him to the core. Made him feel as no woman had ever made him feel…

But…how could he pressure her? He'd been so close in the circle of stones, and then guilt had smashed down hard, driving him back. Seduction was out and telling her the truth would be like holding a gun to her head.

So…

So forget the guilt, try to exert your enormous charm and marry her fast, Charlie told himself. She won't lose by it. Tell her afterwards.

And if she won't marry you?

I won't threaten Tess. The thought was abhorrent.

She's engaged to bloody Donald.

No, she's not. Or if she is, then talk her around. You've got five weeks to do it, Charlie lad.

One week. There's a small matter of a licence. By next Friday.

Okay. One week. So get to work. It has to be worth it. To lose so much if you fail…

Charlie sighed and turned once more to gaze across his land. He stood there for an hour, deep in thought. Then the Earl of Dalston left his battlements and made his way down through his ruined castle. And went to find his lady.

* * *

Charlie returned to Borrowdale mid-morning Saturday and Tess was never more pleased to see anyone. In fact, the way she was feeling, Tess would have welcomed the milkman with open arms and invited him in for coffee. Ghosts or not, the house was getting to her. Cleaning out the echoes of other people's lives…

She'd tackled wardrobes of clothing, packing them up for charity. She'd cleaned and sorted and stored, and negotiated with real estate agents…

She'd worked hard, but there was more to be done. The study containing all the papers still had to be sorted. Tess was about halfway through and was horrified. Christine and her husband seemed to have lived in a soap bubble, where things like life insurance certificates weren't important.

They did have life insurance. Ben was provided for, but Tess found the papers in a heap of documents stuffed down the back of a wardrobe. Probably because the paperwork didn't match the decor!

Charlie walked in and found her sitting on the study floor, sorting out the vast pile and swearing.

'That's not very ladylike.'

Tessa swung round sharply and caught her breath at the sight of him. He'd said he'd be back but…but…but she hadn't expected to feel like this. To be so relieved that she felt like weeping.

And…what on earth was he wearing?

'A kilt,' she managed. 'You're wearing a kilt.'

Charlie was indeed wearing a kilt. But this wasn't a kilt as Tess had seen kilts before—on pipers dressed for ceremonial occasions or playing in highland bands. This was a kilt as it was meant to be worn. It had no adornment. It was a plain, workaday kilt, worn with open-necked shirt with sleeves rolled up above the elbows.

Then there were long socks, and those long, brown, shaggy legs that made Tessa's breath catch in her throat.

She'd never known a kilt could look so blatantly sexy and—what did they say a man wore under his kilt?

'I've come from my highland home,' Charlie told her. He lapsed into an accent that was as broadly Scottish as it was genuine. 'Ma ancestry's Scottish to the core and ma brawny bare legs prove it. Have you missed me, Tessa, ma lass?' Without waiting for an answer, he strode over, scooped her from the floor into his arms and kissed her soundly on the mouth. Deeply. So deeply that she just had to respond.

What *did* a man wear under his kilt?

'I've missed you,' he said, when he could speak at last. When he finally let their mouths part, he released her lips to a distance of about an inch at most. 'Want to go to bed? Now?'

That shook her almost as much as the kiss. Almost shook her out of thinking upward from those brawny knees...

'Charlie Cameron, you put me down this minute!' Tessa's voice was practically a squeak. She wriggled down from his clasp, but even when he obligingly set her on her feet, her knees didn't work the way they were supposed to. She wobbled, and Charlie put his hands on her shoulders to steady her.

'Well?'

She glared up at him, but flooding though her was the knowledge that there was nothing she'd like better than to go to bed with this man. Nothing! Which just showed how divorced the heart could be from the head, she thought crossly, willing her knees not to wobble. She had her whole sensible future mapped out before her, and this man was threatening it all.

Threatening it? He was certainly tempting her. How

would it be—to be a part of this man? Married to Charlie Cameron and his castle…

'Don't be ridiculous,' she managed crossly, and her voice shook a fraction.

'You're not still thinking of marrying Donald?' Charlie demanded. He dropped his big hands onto her waist and held her hard. His fingers nearly encircled her. 'Still? I've left you for three whole days. I was sure you'd see sense by now.'

'Of course I'm marrying Donald.' Tess was trying desperately to make her voice work as it should. If only he'd worn something sensible. Like trousers… Like armour.

'But you just kissed me,' he said reproachfully. 'Oh, Tessa.'

'I did not kiss you.'

He grinned then, a wide, lazy grin that encompassed her heart. 'You did so—and you haven't given me one good reason why you should marry Donald,' he said mildly.

She glared again. 'I love Donald.'

'And what's between you and me is just lust?' Charlie's smile intensified, and his eyes undressed her, right there on the spot. 'Okay, if it's just lust then I can live with that. I'll make do. Do you lust for this woman, from this day forth, in sickness and health, forsaking all others for as long as you both shall lust? The answer, my lovely Tess, is *YES, YES, YES!*'

And Charlie hauled her in so her breasts were crushed against his shirt, so her legs were brushing against his kilt. 'How about it, Tess? Do you lust for me straight back?'

Lust! Lust was nothing to what Tess was feeling. She was on fire from the toes up, and just through the door was Christine's vast bed. And Charlie Cameron was all around her.

But somehow she had to make her head work. She must!

'Charlie, don't be crazy,' she managed, and hauled herself away from his hold. 'If you think I'm marrying a man who wants to marry me just so he can inherit a castle...'

'Castle?'

'Castle!'

'Oh, yeah,' Charlie said blankly. 'I'd forgotten the castle.' He gave a lopsided grin. 'It was the excitement of seeing you again, my love. It made me forget my responsibilities. See? I told you I was in lust.'

Tess took a deep breath, fighting to collect her wits. 'Do you...do you really have to marry in five weeks to inherit your castle?' Tess demanded.

Charlie's grin faded. His face clouded, as if his inheritance was something he'd rather not think about.

'Yeah, I guess...' He dug his thumbs into the waistband of his kilt and looked at her with trouble in his eyes. Dear heaven... The kilt accentuated his masculinity like nothing else could—apart, maybe, from nakedness. The kilt looked just great. *Charlie* looked just great.

'I suppose I do,' he said slowly. Then he brightened. 'Hey, that's two reasons for getting married. The castle *and* lust. Two very good reasons.'

'Donald loves me,' she said belligerently, trying desperately to block out the thought of Charlie's dratted legs. 'That's a better reason.'

'Then I love you, too,' he said promptly. 'Anything Donald can do, I can do better.' Charlie grabbed at her and missed. 'Come here.'

'No.' Tess ducked backward.

'How can you doubt that I love you? You're thc cutest thing on two legs.'

This was way out of line. *Way out.*

'Charlie Cameron, I am not marrying a man who wants me so he can inherit a castle,' Tess stammered. 'It's ridiculous. You'd get your blasted castle and then where would it leave me?'

'In bed?' he said hopefully. 'With me?'

'Oh, yeah? In your castle? There is the small problem of a castle roof...' If he could be ridiculous, then so could she.

'You don't fancy sleeping under the stars?'

'Under the clouds, more like,' she retorted, trying desperately not to chuckle. 'I'm for creature comforts at heart, and I've seen what British summer is like. It's a roof or nothing.'

'I'll build you a roof.' All of a sudden, Charlie's voice was deadly serious. It threw Tessa right off balance. 'It would be my very great honour to build you a roof.'

He made her dizzy...

'I won't marry a man who wears a skirt.'

The grin flashed back. 'Want me to take it off?'

'No!' That was practically a yelp. 'Don't you dare!'

'He who dares, wins.'

'You don't win me.'

'Well, what about Ben?' Charlie continued softly, seeing a chink in her armour and aiming straight for it. 'There's Ben, isn't there, Tess? Who wins Ben? Have you rung Donald about Ben?'

'Of course I have.'

'And does he want him?'

'He doesn't *need* to want him.' Tess put her hands on her hips and looked downright stroppy. It was hard, but somehow she managed it. 'Ben's happy with his grandma. I rang them yesterday and Mrs Blainey says everything's fine.'

'That means Ben's been seen but not heard since you left,' Charlie said flatly. 'I'll bet that's fine by Mrs Blainey, but it's not fine by Ben.'

'This is none...'

'Of my business? I know. You've already told me. Tess, *why* don't you want to marry me?'

It was a crazy question. Totally stupid. But Tess stared up at this crazy, enigmatic man and saw that he wasn't laughing any more. He expected a serious answer.

So what was her serious answer? She had to have one. 'Charlie, Donald wants to marry me for *me*,' she managed. 'Not because if I don't then he'll lose a castle.'

'I'd want to marry you without the castle.'

'Yeah?'

'Yeah,' he said flatly. 'The castle's no big deal.'

'But...the title...'

'I inherit the title anyway,' he told her. 'So you'll be Lady Dalston, regardless.'

'Regardless of whether I marry you or not?'

'Well, that is a difficulty,' he admitted. 'Lady Dalston is sort of expected to be attached in some way to Lord Dalston. I don't know how we can get around that.' He smiled then—not the grin that made it seem as if life was just one long joke, but a smile that was a caress all on its own. A smile of tenderness, and entreaty and understanding, a smile that was within a hair's breadth of her undoing.

'Tess, come and see my castle.' He held out his hand in an imperious gesture. Still the smile, though. Still the tenderness. 'You'll see then that I want to marry you for your own sweet self.'

'You said on the plane that you wanted to marry me because of the castle.'

'That was just a ruse,' Charlie admitted placidly. 'If I'd said I want to marry you because I fell in lust at first sight and love at second, then you'd think I was crazy—now wouldn't you?'

There was just enough seriousness in Charlie's tone to make Tessa stare.

'Of course I would,' she managed. 'But asking me to marry you to save your castle is just as crazy.'

'Is it? Then I'm doomed either way,' he said glumly. 'At least you can see what I'm up against, though.' He took her hand firmly into his, whether she liked it or not. His hold brooked no opposition. 'So now we've known each other for nearly a week and you can see what a great guy I am…'

'I can't see anything of the sort…'

'What a great guy I am,' he repeated firmly. 'Then it's time to come clean. I want to marry you regardless of my castle, Tessa Flanagan. And if you don't believe that, then just come and see the home of my ancestors.'

The road to Charlie's castle was stunning enough. It wound through country that grew more and more rugged—almost as rugged as the Scottish highlands.

'The family originates from Scotland,' Charlie told her. 'I told you. I'm entitled to wear a kilt. Great, great grandpa, give or take a few greats, wandered south of the border, indulged in a spot of pillaging and looting, did a few favours for a king or two—I wouldn't be surprised if we sold out the odd countryman (we Camerons are like that)—and hey presto, we're landed gentry. And when we built our castle, no one was stupid enough to try and take it away from us.'

'Why not?'

'You check out other castles hereabouts,' Charlie told her. 'They have moats and battle scars and fortifications like you wouldn't believe. We didn't need them. We just kept wearing our kilts. The look of our hairy legs had our English and trousered enemies screeching in horror before they as much as thought of pillaging or looting. And they'd have to be tough to get here...'

They certainly would. Tess gazed about the wild and rugged country with awe.

Then Charlie's castle came into view and her heart stood still. It was quite, quite beautiful, but as home sweet home it lacked a little something. It lacked... Well, it lacked everything.

The castle walls still stood, stark stone barriers against the wilderness. There were battlements, with towers on three of the four corners still standing where they'd been built hundreds of years ago. Four massive stone pillars rose before them as they drove toward the vast stone ruin. Once, they must have supported a great sweep of an entrance.

Within the entrance, the castle keep had long disappeared. The forecourt held brambles and fully grown trees and wilderness.

There was little else. Charlie's castle was a vast mound of stone, eerie against the summer sky. It stretched up against the mountains, stern sentinel of ages.

'But it has a great dungeon,' Charlie told her, watching her face for reaction as he parked his car by the stone pillars that once marked the entrance. 'Don't think it's a total ruin. I promised you a roof, my love, and as long as you don't need ventilation we'll do very well. You don't mind a spot of damp, do you, my Tess?' His voice was absurdly anxious.

'Oh, Charlie...' Tess climbed from the car and looked up in awe at Charlie's inheritance. 'Is this what you'll inherit if we marry? What on earth will you do with it?'

'Loan it to the National Trust,' Charlie said promptly. 'Just because I'm such a generous guy.'

'Good grief!' Tess shook her head. 'Is it worth getting married for?'

'I told you, Tess.' Charlie's voice gentled. He came around to her side of the car and took her hand in his. Warmth and strength flowed between them with a force that was almost tangible. 'My castle was an excuse. I want to marry you anyway.'

'Yes, but...' Tess blinked and tried to shake his hand away. There were things going on here that she didn't fully understand. 'What will happen to this if I don't marry you?' she asked. 'You're the next in line, but is there another distant relative waiting in the wings?'

'No.' The gentleness was gone from Charlie's voice now and Tess looked up at him in surprise.

'No? So what will happen?'

'It's entailed,' Charlie said flatly. 'In fact, my uncle can't bequeath it away from me even though his will infers that he can. It just makes it much more complicated. I told you, Tess. Marrying you keeps me away from the lawyers.' His smile returned then. 'So won't you marry me as an act of kindness, my lovely Tess? Marry me to keep me away from the law?'

"I don't...'

'Maybe it was a mistake to bring you here,' Charlie added morosely. 'Maybe I should have left it as a hazy and romantic enticement. Tess, even if it is a ruin, do you fancy being lady of my castle?' He took both her hands then, and Tess had a sudden impression that he was almost afraid.

Afraid of what she'd say?

But he was smiling again. The transient uneasiness passed. 'Before you answer, let me introduce you to our ghosts,' he told her. 'We have some really special ones.'

'I'll just bet you do.'

'Come and meet them,' he said, humour slipping easily back between them. Brooking no protest, he led her inside the confines of the castle wall.

There was a rough path through the brambles and overgrowth in the castle forecourt. Charlie took her along it. As the path ended, steps wound up through the north-east tower. Charlie didn't stop until they were at the highest point of the wall, where a stone door opened out to the battlements. He led her into the sun. Then they stood, high among the ruins of the castle, both of them gazing down at the countryside around them.

'This is my very favourite part of the castle,' Charlie told her.

Tessa could see why. From here she could see for ever. For ever... For ever... Her future...was becoming more obscure by the minute.

'My favourite ghost lives here,' Charlie added.

'Your favourite ghost,' Tess said faintly. 'Complete with clanking armour?'

'Nope.' Charlie grinned. 'My favourite ghost is a lady, and she wears nothing at all.'

'Nothing!' Tess took a deep breath, then she managed a chuckle. 'I should have known. Any favourite of yours would have to be female and naked...' To ask was irresistible, though. 'Go on, then,' she said, goaded. 'Tell me about your ghost.'

'I thought you'd never ask.' Charlie's smile widened. He sat down on the edge of the wall and swung his feet over edge. There was a drop of a hundred or so feet beneath him.

'Is that safe?' Tess asked nervously.

'Yep. It's a bit rotten right over the entrance, but this section is okay. The National Trust has been in recently and checked it, and I figure if it hasn't fallen down in six hundred years it won't fall down now. My lady ghost fell down here, though.'

'How?' Tess sounded suspicious and Charlie laughed up at her.

'You don't sound very trusting.'

'I'm not.'

'I didn't push her. Sit down beside me.'

'I'm not going near that edge in a pink fit.'

'My ghost did.' Charlie looked out over the woods beyond the castle and sighed. 'It's a very romantic story.'

'You have two minutes before I head down to level ground again. This is making me nervous.'

'Okay, okay.' Charlie laughed at her and spread his hands. 'Here goes. Legend has it that my ghost was a lovely lady. Her name was Eleanor and she was just eighteen when she died. She was the daughter of the chief steward here, and she was in love with the third earl. Rumour is he was only seventeen or so and sowing wild oats everywhere he could.'

'Some things stay the same in your family, then,' Tess said darkly and Charlie grinned.

'Yeah, well. So anyway, our boy earl gets called away to fight for his king. He musters his men and he's off to battle. Only the beautiful Eleanor is wild with love and convinced he isn't coming back. He'll die in battle, she screams, and clings to his neck. But our hero—being a man's man—takes no note and rides out through the castle entrance, his men behind him.'

'And then what?' Tess was intrigued. Standing up here, looking out across the wild country surrounding them, she could almost imagine she, too, was like Eleanor. Watching her menfolk march away to war.

'She got desperate,' Charlie said ruefully. 'Maybe she got a bit carried away. She tore up here to see the last of her love, and then, in a frenzy of passion, ripped off all her clothes and stood naked on the highest point. Just a bit further along, where the stones are crumbling now. She screamed to her love to come back—to take her—that she was his.'

Tess stared, astounded. 'She didn't! What a dingbat.'

'You have no soul,' Charlie complained. 'Don't you think that's romantic?'

'I think it's stupid. So then what happened?'

'She fell off,' Charlie said soulfully. He peered over the edge as though expecting to see splattered naked ladies at his feet. 'She died of love.'

'You have to be kidding.'

'Nope. Don't you think she sounds wonderful?'

'Absolutely not. I think she sounds like a fruitcake.'

'Wouldn't you do that for me?'

'In your dreams!'

'Aw, Tess...' Charlie swung his legs around and rose, facing her. His smile was mischievous, and dangerous and tender, all at the same time.

He took a step toward her. And then another.

'Wouldn't you feel just a little something if I was riding away to battle?'

'Yes,' Tess said bluntly. 'Relief.'

'Liar.' He came closer.

'Charlie...'

'Tess, wouldn't you like to marry me and inherit my castle with me?'

'No.'

'Would you like to marry me anyway?' he said anxiously. 'I'm quite happy to give the castle to the National Trust so long as they give me free admission on bank holidays. I don't really want it.'

'Really?'

'Really, Tess,' he said softly and watched her face. 'I want you far more than any castle.'

'That's...that's crazy,' she faltered. 'Charlie, you hardly know me.'

'I know all I need to know.'

'Well, I don't know you. I need time... Donald...'

'Donald is simply a matter of a phone call. Dear Donald. I have made a very great mistake. You are a family friend and I don't marry family friends. I marry lovers. One lover in particular. And I've met my lover. I've met my love. Me, Tess. That's all you have to do. One phone call, and then I'll buy you one ruddy great diamond and then we'll have one ruddy great wedding. And then we'll go to bed. Not necessarily in that order. In fact...'

'In fact, I'm going down,' Tess said hastily. 'This place is going to your head, Charlie Cameron. You're about as sane and sensible as the dear departed Eleanor.'

'I think she's wonderful.'

'All right, she's wonderful,' Tess conceded. 'Very romantic. Find someone like her and marry her.'

'She's a bit dead!'

'What's a little obstacle like that to you?' Tess glared and backed down a couple of steps, putting some distance between her and temptation. 'I have a fiancé and a career on the other side of the world, and you don't think that's an obstacle at all. What's a bit of death to someone really determined?'

'You're taking the mickey out of me,' he complained. 'Really?'

She arched her eyebrows. 'Surely not. Why would you think I'd do something like that? Now I need to go back to Borrowdale, Charlie Cameron. If you won't drive me, then I'll walk.'

'You'd leave me?'

'Got it in one.'

'Tessa, if you walk away from here, I might be tempted to take off all my clothes and holler.'

Tessa caught her breath. The thought of Charlie carrying out his threat was almost irresistible. For one brief moment she let herself think of Charlie Cameron, stark naked and shouting his lungs out for his love from the top of his castle.

She choked.

It was one moment's weakness, though. She couldn't afford another. Somehow she turned her choke into a cough, but Charlie wasn't fooled for a minute.

'Very well,' she said with as much dignity as she could muster. 'Holler away. Only don't slip. Or if you do, do it quietly so I won't have to clean up the mess.'

'You have no soul.'

'That's dead right,' she said with asperity. 'With you around, no girl can afford a soul, Charlie Cameron. It's just too darned dangerous. Now stop this nonsense this minute, Charlie Cameron, and *take me home*!'

Charlie stared down at her for a long, long moment, and Tessa glared back. The moment stretched on and on.

If he followed her... If he took those few short steps now and took her into his arms...then she'd be lost, Tessa thought desperately. She couldn't resist him. She couldn't.

'Charlie...' She faltered and Charlie heard the fear.

The fear was his undoing. What he was doing was immoral, for heaven's sake. Wrong. If she only knew... And suddenly he couldn't bear Tess to know what he'd planned. Nothing could be worth it. Tess... Here was a woman who made him feel as he'd never thought he could feel, and she'd come into his life at such a time...

Impossible. *Impossible!*

So Charlie Cameron closed his eyes for one long moment—and then he opened them and knew what he had to do.

He took his Tessa home.

CHAPTER SEVEN

IT WAS mid-afternoon when Charlie dropped Tessa back to her house. Somehow she'd managed to hold firm to her resolution. She'd been firm that she wanted nothing more to do with him.

'Just drop me back to Borrowdale and then leave,' she'd told him, holding fast to her last vestiges of self-control. 'Please, Charlie...'

He'd heard the quiet desperation in her voice and agreed.

She should have left him at the door. She should... But at the last minute she couldn't bear the parting. Charlie had taken her for a wonderful journey to show her his castle, and it seemed mean not to offer him coffee.

She wanted him gone. But not quite yet...

So Charlie walked into the house beside her, and if he seemed as reluctant—as unsure—as Tessa, then Tess was too disturbed to notice. Tess went to put on the kettle and Charlie stayed alone in the living room.

And paced. He was on new ground. For the life of him, Charlie didn't know what to do. He didn't want this pressure. What he wanted more than anything, he decided, was to slow this down. Back off.

It sounded stupid, but Charlie Cameron, for the first time in his life, seriously cared what a woman thought of him. And his timing was crazy.

If he didn't believe he was starting to love Tessa...if he wasn't starting to feel like a king-sized rat...then this would be so much easier! He'd seen the gamut of emotions running over Tessa's face. He knew that if he took her in his arms now she wouldn't resist—or if she did, then he could break down that resistance. He could sweep her into his arms and make passionate love to her and take her to the altar before she had a chance to change her mind.

Then...if she was angry afterwards, she could divorce him. Legally, though, he'd be married when he turned thirty and the worst of his problems would be solved.

But...the thought of Tessa angry...the thought of Tessa coldly demanding their marriage be dissolved—was beginning to make him feel cold to the core.

So tell her now...

He couldn't. He couldn't put that pressure on her. Because, more than anything in the world, Charlie was starting to realize that he wanted her to marry him for *him.* He'd started this as a semi-serious joke and the joke was losing its humour by the minute. So now he wanted Tess to marry him thinking the only thing at stake was a mouldering castle and nothing else...

What a mess! There wasn't even time to think! Charlie raked his fingers through his hair and swore under his breath. He needed time and so did she. Tess needed time to sort herself out—realize just how dreadful the dreadful Donald was. Even go back to Australia and have it out face to face with the man. For Charlie to follow and let matters take their course. As they surely would...

There was no time at all. *He needed a bride by Friday.*

So Charlie wandered restlessly around the living room and wondered what the hell to do next.

'The phone answer machine's flashing,' he called. 'Do you want me to play your messages?'

Tess frowned. She'd rung Donald the day before. She

knew he wouldn't be wasting money ringing her again. So who was it?

Maybe it was someone for her sister or brother-in-law. Someone who didn't know about their death. If so...

'Yes, please,' she called gratefully.

Silence while Charlie hit the replay button. The kettle whistled and died, and then a girl's uncertain voice filled the room, reaching out to the kitchen beyond. There was no mistaking the voice. It was Emma, Ben's nanny.

'Miss... Tessa... I don't know your last name.' The voice was faltering and unsure. 'I dunno whether you're staying in the Borrowdale house or not, but I just sort of hope you might be. I'm ringing...I'm ringing to let you know I've been sacked.'

She paused and her distress filled the room before she started to speak again. 'You see...the old dragon didn't like me from the start. Only Ben screamed his head off when Mrs Blainey tried to take him away so she had to bring me here. But I don't fit what she thinks a nanny ought to be. I play my music too loud. She hates my clothes and my hair and she doesn't like me and Ben giggling. And...well, this morning she kicked me out.'

The girl paused again. Her uncertainty that she was talking to anyone at all was obvious.

'Miss... Tessa, if you can hear this, I just gotta say that Ben'll be *so* unhappy. She dresses him up and shows him off to her friends but he's not allowed to make a noise or anything. And this morning...before I left, another nanny arrived from the agency and she's *awful*. She's old and crabby and she told Ben off for making a noise five minutes after she'd met him. Just the pits. But Mrs Blainey *likes* her.'

'Anyway...' The girl's voice trailed away. 'There's nought I can do. I'm catching a train back to Keswick to my mum's place. My stepdad's away so I can stay there for a few days. If you want to contact me...' She read out a phone number. 'But I hope you can do something. I'm that fond of him...'

Her voice broke on a sob and the connection was cut.

Silence. Charlie turned to find Tess in the doorway and her face was white as death.

'Well?' he said softly.

Tess closed her eyes. 'I *knew* she was awful.'

'Emma?'

'No. Mrs Blainey.'

'And yet you left him...'

'I know I left him,' she snapped. 'But he had Emma.'

'He doesn't have Emma now,' Charlie said quietly, watching her face. 'He has a dragon of a grandmother and, if Emma's to be believed, a dragon of a new nanny. What will you do, Tess?'

'I'll have him. Of course I'll have him. I'll go and fetch him now.'

'And Donald?

'Donald's just going to have to lump it,' Tess said grimly, and her pale face was set. She looked up at Charlie, her eyes pleading. 'Charlie, could you take me to the railway station. Please?'

'There's no train from Keswick. You'd have to catch a bus to Penrith and then...'

'Stop quibbling,' she snapped. 'The bus station, then. You're wasting time.'

'Then you stop quibbling,' Charlie told her. His face was as set as hers. Every inch as determined. 'If you think I'm letting you face dragons alone, then you're very much mistaken. Ben's three years old and he's alone. If it takes two of us to get him out of that house, then he'll have us both. You're coming with me, Tessa, lass. In my car.'

'But...'

'Don't 'but' me, Tessa,' he told her. 'I might be forced to take myself out of your life, my love, but this is Ben we're talking about. We're facing Ben's dragons together.'

They heard Ben as soon as they arrived at Mrs Blainey's home.

Charlie parked by the railings near the front door and, as they emerged from the car, a child's desolate sobs reached out to them from the window above.

'There's nothing else,' a woman's voice snapped. 'You eat your egg or you'll go to bed hungry.'

'I want Emma...' It was a voice that had almost given up hope. Tess didn't need to be told that Ben had been sobbing for hours.

'Emma's gone.' Another voice—Mrs Blainey's. 'You'll just have to get used to doing things *my* way from now on. She's gone for good. Enough of this nonsense. Put him to bed, Mrs West. The child's been too much indulged and he's bound to be difficult for a few days.'

'He's eaten nothing.'

'Then let him go hungry. He'll learn.'

Let him go hungry. *Her nephew*...

She'd heard enough. Tess had no need of her dragon slayer accomplice. She had no need of anyone. Charlie was left behind. She was up the steps in seconds, and ringing the bell as if her life depended on it. The maid opened the door and this time it was Tess who shoved her foot in the door and pushed her way into the house before the woman could argue.

'I want Ben,' she said harshly. 'Get him for me.'

The maid goggled. 'Mrs Blainey's not...'

'Don't give me that nonsense,' Tess snapped, and headed up the stairs two at a time.

And Charlie, coming mildly after, gave the maid a rueful grin and followed. Clearly Tessa didn't need him, but he wasn't staying downstairs for quids.

Upstairs, Tess opened three doors before she found Ben. They were all still in the room set up as the nursery—Ben, Mrs Blainey and the Mrs West whom Charlie figured had to be the new nanny. He followed Tess into the room and watched in appreciation as Tess walked straight over to where her little nephew was sagging on his high, hard chair. A congealing egg sat before him.

Tess ignored it. She ignored the women. Charlie thought she didn't even see them. She had eyes only for the tiny, tear-stained little boy, still dressed in his ridiculous Lord Fauntleroy suit. She lifted Ben straight up into her arms and held him close.

'Oh, Ben… It's okay. I'm here now. I shouldn't have left you. Hush…'

Ben hiccuped into her shoulder and, to Tessa's astonishment, he wrapped his arms round her neck like he was drowning.

'Mummy…'

With his Emma gone, he saw the likeness. Tess was like his mother. He might still want his Emma but, given the choice between a mother substitute and a grandmother like Mrs Blainey, there was no choice. He clung and clung and wriggled his small body just as close as he could get.

Save me, his body language said, and Tess turned to face Mrs Blainey like a tigress with her cub.

'How dare you dismiss Emma?' she said fiercely, cradling the sobbing child close against her. 'How dare you sack Emma? Emma's all Ben has.'

'Miss Flanagan...!' Margot Blainey's voice swelled with outrage. 'How dare *you*...?'

'That's my line.' Tessa's glare deepened. 'I want his clothes. Now. We're leaving. Charlie's taking us home.' She put her hand up to run her fingers through the little boy's hair. 'Don't cry, Ben love. I'm doing what I should have done four days ago. I'm not your mummy but I'm your Aunty Tess and I love you just like your mummy did. I'll take you home and then we'll see if we can't find your Emma for you.'

Mrs Blainey's eyes flashed fire. Shock fading, she drew herself up to full autocratic height and let her bosom swell.

'This is nonsense. You can get out of my house, girl,' she snapped. 'Right now. I've dismissed Emma and she's gone for good.'

'You have no right to dismiss Ben's nanny.'

Charlie leaned back against the wall and folded his arms across his chest. He'd come prepared to fight on Tessa's behalf. There was no need, no need at all.

'I'm Ben's legal guardian and I'm taking him home,' Tess was saying. 'You have no power to stop me.'

'You can't.'

'She can,' Charlie said mildly. 'Like she says, Tessa's Ben's legal guardian.'

The woman wheeled on Charlie.

'And who are you? You haven't even had the decency to introduce yourself. Acting for Tessa, I believe you said. Does that make you a lawyer? If you are, then you know that you're trespassing...'

Charlie slowly straightened. It was his turn now to put on the aristocratic bit. Heck, the sooner they got out of this place the better. This lady gave him the shivers, and if flashing a bit of title could speed things up...

'If I haven't introduced myself then maybe I've been

remiss,' he said smoothly. 'I'm Lord Charles Cameron—thirteenth Earl of Dalston.' He dug into his breast pocket and handed over one of the cards Henry had had printed for him. Hey, this was twice they'd proved useful.

'I have lawyers and resources to fight you on any level you care to choose,' he added mildly. 'And I know Tessa's rights. So I wouldn't make a fuss.' He watched Margot Blainey's jaw drop with a nod of satisfaction as she read his business card. 'So please, collect his things, *there's a good woman*. And we'll be going.'

He gave her his blandest, blue-blood smile as Tessa stared across at him in astonishment. She could practically see the first twelve earls of his family lining up at his shoulder.

'You... She...' Mrs Blainey gasped. 'You're not... I don't believe you. And she...' She pointed an accusatory finger at Tessa. 'She hasn't got the resources to care for my grandchild.'

'I have any resources you care to name,' Charlie said gently. 'And Tessa's marrying me.'

'She's not engaged to you. She's engaged to someone called Donald...'

'You *have* been doing your homework,' Charlie approved. 'Very good. But unfortunately your information's out of date. Donald's last week's boring news. As of now, we're a family, Tess and Ben and I. See if you can split us up. If you dare.'

And he gave her another blue-blood smile—aristocracy bestowing favours on the peasantry—then gathered Tessa and Ben before him and ushered them out of the room.

'Take Ben out to the car, Tess,' he told her at the door. 'I'll stay and collect his things. I don't think Mrs Blainey has any more objections at all.'

* * *

It was a weird night.

Charlie drove them back to Borrowdale, with Tess cradling Ben in the rear seat. They had no child restraint. In fact, it would have been safer to stay in Newcastle for the night, but Tess decided Ben would be better off in his own home, in his old bedroom. Too much had happened to this small boy in the last couple of weeks to put any more pressures on him.

Tess could only be grateful for Charlie's presence. She was in no mood to argue with him, nor could she resist Charlie's further help. Maybe she could have stayed in a hotel in Newcastle, but when Charlie ushered them into the back seat of his car and nosed the Jaguar back to the Lake District, she could only feel relief.

Ben clung and clung. Charlie tried ringing Emma on his mobile phone, but the number she'd given rang out. For tonight, they were on their own.

Charlie and Tess... They were all Ben had.

The enormity of what had happened was just starting to dawn on Tess. There was no going back now. Ben was her responsibility and, with her face nestled into the little boy's crop of curls and his sleepy arms entwined around her neck, she'd have it no other way.

But it scared the life out of her.

'You'll have to marry me now,' Charlie said conversationally and Tessa gave a start.

'What?'

'You'll have to marry me.'

Like...we'll have to go to the launderette tomorrow. Just as pragmatic.

'Why?'

'You have a child. Being a single mum is no fun at all.'

'Yeah? How do you know?'

'Don't sound so suspicious,' Charlie complained.

'You make it sound like I've scattered my seed across the world, leaving a trail of single mums wherever I go.'

'I didn't mean...'

'I know you didn't.' He smiled into the fading light. 'I've told you, Tess. I'm a thoroughly nice guy. Husband material, in fact and, believe it or not, you're the very first lady I've offered myself to.' He chuckled. 'In marriage, that is.'

'Yeah, right...'

'Scout's honour.'

She did believe him. Plausible or not, she did believe. But...

'Then why do you want to marry me now?' The light was almost gone. They'd stopped at Penrith and bought fish and chips—Ben had been persuaded to eat a paper bag full of chips and Tess was in no mood to worry about whether it was good for him or not—and now he was so close to sleep that Tess knew he wasn't listening. The sound of her voice—so like his mother's—was a comfort and a lullaby by itself.

'I told you. I'm in love.'

Tess shook her head. 'I don't believe you.'

'I'm in lust?' His voice was hopeful.

'Charlie, be serious.'

'I am being serious,' he told her, and his voice suddenly was, deadly serious. 'There's all sorts of reasons I want to marry you. Believe it or not, you're carrying one in your arms right now.'

'What, Ben?' Tess looked down, startled. 'You're not serious. You can't really want Ben.'

'I do.'

It was the truth. Charlie's feelings of anger at the little boy's plight had surprised him in their intensity. There was no way he'd let the kid return to Margot Blainey's cold house. He wouldn't mind having a kid like Ben to call his own, to take care of and watch grow...

But also... How to tell Tessa that Ben made him feel less guilty? That this marriage wouldn't be just for Charlie now. He could give as well as gain, so when Tess finally discovered the truth...

'Charlie...' Tessa's voice was troubled.

'Look, let's go home and put Ben to bed, shall we?' Charlie said gently. 'And then let's sit down and discuss this.' His voice brightened. 'Or maybe even lie down...'

'I don't...'

'Leave it, Tess,' Charlie said and his voice was suddenly harsh. 'Leave it. Until tonight.'

The lights were dimmed when Tessa finally came downstairs. Charlie had left her to put Ben to bed, but Ben had woken fully when she'd tried to leave, and clung.

Tessa had cuddled him and crooned him to sleep, using lullabies and comforts she'd dredged up from her own childhood long ago. It was weird, she thought, sitting in the dark with the little boy. She was a nurse. She was used to calming frightened children, but the feelings she had for Ben were astounding her. It was as if he were already her own child.

Maybe it was because she and Christine were identical twins. Christine had always felt part of her, and Ben was part of Christine.

For whatever reason, Ben clung to her as his own and she clung right back.

Whatever happened now in this whole stupid mess, she and Ben were in this together.

And Charlie? He wouldn't be left out of the equation. But how could three people who'd just met equal one instant family? She walked downstairs and found Charlie waiting for her, a glass of champagne in his hand. She looked at it with distrust.

'To celebrate,' he said softly. 'I found it in the cellar and there'll never be a better reason to celebrate. We've just become a family.'

'Charlie...'

She looked up at him with eyes that were fearful and he pressed the glass into her hand. Once again, he had that savage jolt of guilt. He was pushing her too hard, far too hard. He had her in a corner and he knew it.

'Donald...'

'Ring Donald now,' he said, watching her face. 'Tell him what you've done.'

'It doesn't matter,' Tess said miserably. 'Even if Donald doesn't want Ben, I'm still caring for him.'

'What will you do?'

'I'll go home.' Tess took a deep breath. 'To Australia. There's child care at the hospital where I work. Ben can go there...'

'He needs permanence. He needs time to know and trust you. He doesn't need child care.'

'Well, what would you have me do?' Tess flashed. 'I can't afford not to work. There's enough money to care for Ben but I won't use his money on me. If you think I'm living a life of idleness on Ben's money...'

'I figure that's what Mrs Blainey intended.'

'Well, I'm not Mrs Blainey.'

'No. You're not.' Charlie gave up on the champagne. He lifted the glass from her nerveless fingers and set it on the mantle, with his. 'On second thoughts, maybe the champagne can wait.'

'Charlie, no...' She could see from his face what he intended. Tess backed, her hands spread before her. 'I don't want this.'

'You don't want me?'

'I don't know you,' she said desperately. 'I mean... You're a lord, for heaven's sake. And...and heaven knows what else. It doesn't make any sense that you're bulldozing me into marriage.'

'It makes sense to me. You're the most beautiful...'

'You've had "beautiful",' she snapped. 'Don't tell me you haven't. You can get "beautiful" in hundreds of places. Someone with your looks and your money and your...'

'My castle?' He was laughing at her! 'Are you saying any girl would swoon at my feet because of my castle?'

'This is nonsense,' she whispered. 'Charlie, I don't know you and you don't know me.'

'I know you have the best right hook in the business.' Charlie smiled. 'You know I'm still carrying bruises. That's why I want Ben. I suspect you've damaged me for life and I'm not going to father a son any other way.'

'Well, you're not...'

'Tessa, shut up,' he said softly. 'Come here.'

'Why don't you just say, "Come here, *there's a good woman*," and be done with it?' she managed.

Charlie grinned. 'I did enjoy saying it,' he admitted. 'But I have a feeling that earls who make a habit of saying it end up with socialist mutiny on their hands. And socialist mutiny is the last thing I need right now.' He held out his hands toward her. 'So Tess, my love...please...come here.'

She didn't, not at once. She stared up at him with eyes that were baffled and wary but...but sort of hopeful, allowing just a glimmer of hope that he might be serious. That he might just want her for her own sweet self.

It was enough. Charlie saw the glimmer of hope in her eyes and Charlie moved. It was a second kiss, and it headed straight for that defiant glimmer of hope. It ignored the fear. It ignored the confusion. It just built on the hope there was, and searched for more. And there was more.

Of course there was more. Tessa's body had been yearning for almost a week now, regardless of what her head had been telling her. It had been screaming that here was a man whom she'd never thought existed.

Tessa had never had much interest in the male of the species. Her father had walked out on them early and her mother had lumped all males into the 'useful for propagating the species but not much else' basket. Donald had been useful as a friend as well, and Yaldara Bay was just too small for Tess to experiment.

But now... It was as if all the experiments she should have tried over the past ten years were packed right here into one powerful punch. Charlie's body right against hers. Charlie's arms wrapping her tight against him and holding hard. His hand cupping her chin, forcing her to look up at him.

And then his mouth on hers.

Nothing else. Short circuits—fusing—call it what you will. There was nothing else but Charlie. The feel of him, the smell of him, the sheer, arrant maleness of him.

He was impossible to resist, even if she'd wanted to. Tessa's lips opened under his and her hands wrapped around him and held hard—hauling the hardness of his chest against her breasts. She felt herself arch against him—heard herself whimper with wanting. There was nothing but him. Nothing...

And her thighs were on fire with wanting.

Fire...

Good grief. The word flashed though her head and she almost laughed. She'd read of sexual fire in women's magazines—of heat and flame in lovemaking—and decided they were fantasy land, a description women made up to keep men happy. Certainly she'd felt nothing remotely resembling heat and flames with Donald.

Yet here she was, holding Charlie's body close to hers, and her body was heating up as if there were an internal combustion engine right inside. Her thighs were moving of their own volition—and she was so empty she could scream.

Charlie's kilt was brushing against her legs and his fingers were playing with the zipper of her jeans and...and...

She writhed. She writhed against him and, with a triumphant moan, Charlie lifted her high.

'Where to, my lovely Tess?' He gazed around them—through to the big bed beyond the living room.

But it was her sister's bed. They both knew that, and it wasn't right. Even the thought of it made the flame die down a little. A little, a very little.

'Wait. We'll have to wait.' There was almost a groan of desperation in Charlie's voice. His need was as urgent as hers. Charlie carried her through to the kitchen and set her down on a chair by the stove. 'Don't move,' he ordered in a voice that cracked with passion. 'Not one inch.'

Then he left her, with Tessa's body craving to follow. Her head was drifting through a haze of want and want and want...

He was back, carrying a vast armload of quilting. Charlie spread it on the floor before the lovely Aga. Back again for mounds of pillows. And then he came to her again, his eyes dark with passion, as he pulled her up to stand before him.

'The kitchen's the heart of the house,' he murmured. 'And you're my heart. Can I undress you, my love?

She couldn't speak. She could only look at him with

eyes that were as dark as his. There was no mistaking the message they gave him.

So slowly, tenderly—reverently—he undressed her. He unfastened the buttons on her blouse one by one and lifted the blouse away, and then stood back to savour the sight of her.

Tess lifted her hands behind her and unfastened the hook on her bra. It fell to the floor.

Charlie closed his eyes and his kilt moved. All on its own...

He came back to her then. Gently his hands ran around the firm warm swell of her breasts, savouring the feel of them. Wanting them. Loving them. And then the zipper of her jeans was somehow undone and her jeans were sliding to the floor, still attached to her wisp of lace panty—and she was naked before him and proud of it.

She had never felt so good in all her life. So sure that what she was doing was right. She arched her body upright, glorying in her nakedness. Glorying in her wantonness.

Wanting...

There was joy running through and through at the expression in Charlie's eyes. He was loving her. He was glorying in her as much as she was glorying in him.

Standing apart. Savouring the moment.

'Charlie...' There was love and laughter in her voice.

'Yes, my love?' His voice was husky, deep and gravelly and naked with passion.

'Isn't it about time you showed me what a man wears under his kilt?' She eyed the heavy tartan and her eyes twinkled. 'It's trying to get out all by itself.'

Charlie's eyes widened and flared. With a swoop of triumphant laughter he lunged at her and swung her high into his arms, claimed her, possessed her, and there was no turning back.

He was a lord and she was his lady. His...

They were falling backwards onto the wonderful bed he'd made beside the big, warm Aga, and the kilt was gone and the shirt and the long socks on those long, long muscled legs...

He was as naked as Tess, and he was holding her—skin against skin—as if she was the most precious thing in the entire world. But he wasn't close enough. Still he wasn't close enough.

Her body was screaming for him, wanting him, aching for him with a yearning that was irresistible. She rolled in his arms and up, so her body was over his and she pulled her head back from his and gazed down at him and all the love in her heart was clear in her eyes...

'Charlie Cameron,' she said softly. 'My lord...'

She lifted her hips...lifted so she could feel his manhood just where she wanted him to be...and she drove down hard to take him into her.

Life could have ended right at that moment.

There are some moments in life so good—so wonderful that to describe them is impossible. Orgasm...the word wasn't big enough, not wonderful enough. Fire and flame and tempest.

Charlie moving inside her, rolling her over so it was now he who was setting the pace. Stroke after stroke of rhythmic magic, slicked bodies and laughter and wonder and love.

And then the climax—the earth-shattering moment when Tessa thought the world must surely end because nothing could be as good as this again. Nothing....

Charlie...

Only Charlie.

And then the realization that it was finished—over—

but he was still inside her and it didn't have to end here. There was all night before them. And morning.

And the rest of their lives?

Tess lay, exhausted and wondrous, cradled in her lover's arms and feeling the beat of his heart against hers, and she knew that whatever happened now, this had no ending.

'Marry me,' Charlie murmured at some time during that wondrous night and Tessa had nothing to say but, 'Yes.'

Marry him? She was already married.

Her soul belonged to this man for ever.

CHAPTER EIGHT

AT SIX the next morning Tess disentangled herself from her lover's arms and went to make a phone call.

She wrapped herself in a blanket and padded across to the living room door, then she turned back to look at her love.

Charlie slept on. His dark face was peaceful against the pillows, his arm still flung across the bedclothes where she'd been lying. If he stayed right where he was, then in a few minutes she could crawl back against him, that arm would tighten around her and she'd be his.

But first... Back home it was three o'clock on a Sunday afternoon. Donald would be watching football replays on television. He didn't like his football interrupted, but at least he should be alone. And if she didn't ring...

She looked back at Charlie and knew that, whatever happened now, she couldn't marry Donald. What she felt for Donald was a pale travesty of what love could be.

What she felt for Charlie was a life force sweeping through and through her. She could only hope that one day Donald would feel the same force within him—would meet someone who could stir him as Charlie stirred her.

So she took a deep breath and went to interrupt Donald's football.

Charlie wasn't asleep.

He'd felt her stir and let her go, knowing instinctively what she intended. Now he listened in the quiet of the dawn and heard her break off her engagement to this man called Donald.

It didn't take much.

'Something's happened,' he heard her say and then there was a long silence.

'Yes, part of it's Ben. I want to take care of him, Donald, but...'

Silence again.

'Donald, I *am* keeping him with me. But even if I wasn't...'

In the end, she didn't have to explain about Charlie. At the end of what must have been a long tirade, she said one more thing.

'I'm sorry you feel like that about it, Donald, but maybe it's just as well. I wish you all the best for the future, but your future doesn't include me.' And Tess put the phone down.

Charlie lay in silence, waiting for her to come back to bed. She didn't come at once. Instead he heard her cross to the window and stand, staring out across the peaceful surface of Derwent Water.

Dear heaven, he loved her. He'd never imagined he could feel like this about a woman, never dreamed it could be this good. He felt his body stir at the thought of her and he wanted more than anything else to lunge across to the living room and take her in his arms and haul her back into his bed, into his body.

She *had* to marry him. She must. And not just because of what he would lose. Should he tell her? And risk her walking away? Losing her as well? Losing everything?

So much was at stake.

Charlie stared bleakly up at the ceiling and tried to make a choice, and couldn't. He couldn't tell her. He was pressuring her enough.

Let her marry him for *him*. Please. For love. And the rest...the rest must just take care of itself.

After they were married.

The morning sun across Derwent Water was beautiful. Tessa gazed across the peaceful waters and felt her heart settle within her. This was right. Charlie was right. Here she was more at home than she'd ever been in her life.

How had she ever agreed to marry Donald in the first place? she wondered. He was like a habit—a habit started as a child and now as familiar and comfortable as an old pair of socks. But one didn't marry an old pair of socks. Especially when the socks rejected your little nephew utterly.

Especially when you didn't love...

Donald had made it easy for her—not wanting Ben, she thought thankfully. She could walk away without a pang, and turn to Charlie.

Charlie.

She heard him stir and seconds later he came up behind her. His arms wrapped around her waist and the blanket around her shoulders slipped to the floor. He was as naked as she was. Charlie pulled her in against him so her spine was curved against his chest, two bodies moulded into one.

'Exit Donald, stage left?' he asked quietly, and she didn't have to answer. He kissed her tousled curls.

'Tess, I have something for you. Want to see?' he asked her, and he pulled her around to face him. She swung into his body naturally, her breasts against his, her heart linking to his, and she looked down to see what he held in his hand.

'I strongly object to naked women,' he said softly, tenderly—and he lifted the lid of a tiny crimson box nestled in his palm. 'So I decided to do something about it.'

A diamond glinted and twinkled in the morning light. One solitary diamond on a thin band of gold. One diamond so exquisite it took her breath away.

'You'll never go naked again,' Charlie said softly, slipping it onto the third finger of her left hand. 'I want you to wear this, my lovely Tess. For ever and ever and ever.'

He kissed her deeply on the mouth, so deeply that the world stopped spinning. Everything stopped, except the beating of Charlie's heart.

But, when she finally was released—allowed one tiny fraction of an inch to let her breathe—Tessa's eyes were faintly troubled.

'Charlie, I don't know...'

'Don't know?' He cupped her chin and tilted her face to look at her. 'What don't you know?'

'It's all so rushed. Are you sure? You know nothing about me.'

'I know I love you.'

'I love you too,' she said simply. 'But Charlie...what if you change your mind?'

'I'm not going to change my mind,' he told her, and his voice was deadly serious. 'I want to marry you, whether you'll marry me now or marry me in a year's time. But I want you *now*, Tessa.'

'But...you still want to marry me before your birthday?'

'If you'll have me.'

'And afterwards... Please, it's not just because of the castle? Promise me, Charlie?'

That was easy. 'I promise,' he said firmly in a voice that brooked no doubts. 'I promise on my honour, Tessa Flanagan, Tessa soon to be Cameron. I swear to you that I want to marry you, regardless. But...' He smiled and his smile had the power to twist her inside out, to make her do anything in the wide world that this man asked of her. 'You will marry me now, though, Tess?'

'If you think...'

'I think.' He kissed her again. 'As we're getting married anyway, it does seem stupid not to do it soon.' He smiled, his slow, lazy, seductive smile, and his hold on her naked skin tightened. His body was craving hers and she could feel it. 'We'll keep the lawyers at bay and we'll be married into the bargain. Hell, Tess, we're married anyway.'

'We're not married.'

'I feel married. Don't you?'

'I...'

'You'd better feel married.' He put a finger against her lips and ran it slowly over her teeth. The sensation was spine-tingling, thigh-consuming. Tessa's internal combustion engine was running on red hot. Any minute now it'd explode. 'For a start, were you protected last night?'

'Protected...' Tessa stared, trying to think despite the erotic feel of Charlie's body against hers. What was he asking? Protected? And then she figured what he was talking about. 'Oh, help. I suppose... Oh, help...'

'See? We're married already.' Charlie's voice was triumphant. 'So let's make it legal. I want no base-born toddlers cluttering up the family tree. It sullies our entries into the peerage no end.' He kissed her again, his hands lifting her body right off the ground—and then sweeping her high into his arms to deepen the kiss. 'I'd like lots of entries, but I'd like the first one to be our marriage. Agreed, my love?'

'Charlie...'

'No more niggles,' he told her firmly in a voice that was laced with passion. 'I refuse to listen to niggles. Tessa, today I think we should find Emma for Ben and then tomorrow take you into Penrith, see my lawyer and find out what we have to do to get ourselves married—and then buy you a wedding dress. The most beautiful wedding dress in the world. Maybe even go to London to find a dress. Before you can even think about changing your mind. How about *that* for a plan?'

His hold tightened even further, his grip on her was taking her breath away. Charlie was taking her breath away.

'We could go back to Australia and marry if you like,' he told her huskily, as if still in thought between kisses. Though how he could think with this *frisson* of electricity charging back and forth… 'Face our friends—then take ourselves up to the Great Barrier Reef for a honeymoon.'

'But…' Amazingly she was able to think, just a little bit—but it was a very important thought. 'But Ben…'

'We'll take Emma and Ben with us. I'll bet Emma would love a north Queensland honeymoon.'

'But…' Tess hauled herself back a whole two inches from his face. 'Charlie, it'll cost you a fortune.'

'I have a fortune,' he said seriously. 'Didn't I tell you? I'm seriously rich. And with you in my arms, my lovely Tessa, then I'm the richest man in all the world. There's only one thing I need to complete my happiness…one thing…'

'What's…?'

She didn't finish. She couldn't. A light blazed behind Charlie's eyes that told Tess exactly what he needed right now to make him the richest man in the world.

And Tessa needed it too.

Right now.

Ben found them an hour later.

He hiked into the kitchen with a battered teddy under

his arm, stopped at the door, stuck his thumb in his mouth and surveyed the tumbled bedclothes on the floor with astonishment.

'Is this a cubby house?' he asked.

Tessa opened her eyes and stirred in Charlie's arms, but Charlie was already awake.

'Yep.' He shifted sideways in the makeshift bed, taking Tessa with him, not letting her out of his hold. 'Want to come in?'

Slow consideration. Tess smiled at her little nephew and she shoved her lover twelve inches apart from her. She could feel Charlie's reluctance to let her go even an inch, but her shove was unrelenting. If Charlie wanted them to be a family, then he'd just have to learn what a family was.

'Come into the middle,' she said. 'It's warmest. And Teddy can come too.'

Ben stood at the door for two long minutes, clutching Teddy as if life depended on it. But Tess and Charlie lay placidly side by side in their wonderful bed, and smiled at him and put no pressure on at all—and finally it was all just too inviting.

Ben took one tentative step forward—and then another—and then a fast scramble until he was right under the bedclothes between them.

Teddy, too.

The pair snuggled down with just two noses peeping out from under the covers.

'Can we have breakfast in our cubby?' he asked breathlessly.

'Yep.' Charlie's big arm came round and hooked Ben and Tess and Teddy in his grasp. 'That's a great idea. Toast with honey. Honey holds the crumbs together.'

But Ben was making a discovery. 'You've got no pyjamas on,' he said accusingly, and hitched his own flannels up in virtuous indignation.

'Heck, are you the only respectable person in this cubby?' Charlie shook his head in disgust. 'There's only one thing for it, our Ben. You and Teddy will just have to make the toast.'

'Silly. I can't make toast.' And Ben giggled.

Ben's giggle. It was the first time Tess had heard it and it was the sweetest sound. The best!

Maybe this was right, Tess thought happily, dreamily. Maybe dreams did come true and they could be a family.

'Mummy never lets me make messes downstairs,' Ben announced. 'I've never ever had a cubby house in the kitchen before.'

'Tessa likes cubbies in the kitchen,' Charlie told him.

'How do you know?' Tess demanded. She was feeling almost deliriously happy. Toe-curlingly happy.

'I just know,' Charlie said definitely. 'And I know because that's just the sort of lady your Aunty Tess is, Ben, lad.'

'What, messy?' Tess demanded. That was a pretty weak try at indignation, Tess thought, but she didn't really care.

'Nope. Not messy. Happy.' Charlie's arm tightened around all of them. 'Ben, how would you like to keep living with your Aunty Tess and with me? Would that be okay?'

Ben snuggled down further. 'I might,' he said cautiously. 'I like cubbies.' And then he frowned. 'But Emmy's not here.'

'No. We'll have to try and find her for you.'

'I like living with Emmy.'

'Then I hope Emmy likes living with us.'

'Charlie...' Tess put her own arm around her little nephew and held him close, as though defending him from trouble. 'Charlie, can I...can we afford Emma? I mean, really? Nannies are expensive.'

'I told you, Tessa,' Charlie said placidly and he grinned like the cat who'd finally found his cream. *All* his cream. A whole full milk tanker of cream! 'I told you, Tess Flanagan. With you by my side, I can afford anything. Anything at all.'

They had a very silly day. A nothing day. A day of playing silly games with Ben and making his small body relax. Of letting him forget his troubles. Of making life seem normal. That meant having toast in bed, and then sandwiches on the back lawn for lunch and spending the afternoon puddling round at the water's edge with toy boats and sticks and far too much mud.

'I'm sure you have much more important things to be doing,' Tess told Charlie dubiously, but his eyes blazed at her and they twinkled with laughter and her own passion and happiness was reflected right back at her.

'I'm building a family,' he told her. 'Nothing else counts.'

They finally contacted Emma late that night. She was overjoyed to hear from them and they agreed to collect her from Keswick the following afternoon.

'That's good,' Charlie announced. 'We have business in Penrith tomorrow. We can kill two birds with one stone. Or maybe three?'

'Business?'

'If we're to be married by my birthday, then we have to register our intentions by this Friday,' Charlie told her. Ben was safely tucked into bed again and Charlie had Tess right where he wanted her. Between sheets. He held her close and kissed her. 'I've got my bride by Friday...'

'That's me, isn't it?' she whispered. 'A bride by

Friday.' Once more that shaft of doubt swept over her. 'You really did have to find a bride by Friday.'

'Only to keep the lawyers at bay,' Charlie said contentedly. 'I have everything I ever wanted in life, now. I can't ask for more.'

He kissed her again. And again. And after that, there was no room to voice any doubts at all. They made wonderful, passionate love and Charlie drifted off to sleep with Tessa held close to his heart.

But Tess lay awake and stared into the dark. And wondered. Wondered what would have happened if she'd met Charlie after Friday.

On Monday they met Charlie's lawyer in Penrith.

Edwin Roberts was about as different from Tessa's first experience with English lawyers as it was possible to be. He greeted Tess with real warmth and his warmth extended to Ben, clinging to Tessa's hand.

'I'm delighted to meet you, my dear,' he told her, and when Charlie explained what they wanted his delight knew no bounds.

'Oh, my lord...this is *most* satisfactory. If I might say so, I couldn't have wished for a better outcome.'

Tess frowned. 'But...doesn't this mean we're doing you out of business?'

'Business?' The lawyer looked out at Tess from under bushy grey eyebrows. 'I don't understand.'

'I told Tess if she didn't marry me then the legal bit was a nightmare,' Charlie said easily. 'I would have ended up paying you a fortune.'

The lawyer smiled.

'Well, maybc you would have, my lord. I agree. But it's business I don't mind doing without, I assure you.'

Tessa gritted her teeth. Suddenly she had to know, she had to have confirmation.

'If I don't marry Cha...Lord Dalston,' she said and cast a sideways glance at Charlie, as if apologizing for her need to verify what he'd told him. 'He... Does Charlie still inherit everything?'

But the lawyer didn't hesitate. 'Oh, undoubtedly,' he said smoothly. 'Eventually everything comes to him, regardless of his uncle's wishes. Lord Dalston... Charles...is the sole heir. There's no disputing that at all. It's only... The terms of the will make it so difficult, you understand. It just causes so much trouble and not just for...'

'Yes, well...' Charlie swung Ben up into his arms and directed a quelling glance at his lawyer. 'Enough of that. We're here to register for marriage, Mr Roberts. We want to marry in Australia a month from today. Can you organize that?'

'Of course I can.' The lawyer rubbed his hands together with delight. 'Nothing would make me happier.'

The conversation moved smoothly to the legal requirements of their wedding. Enough of Tessa's doubts. She'd had her assurance, she had to be satisfied.

After leaving the elderly lawyer—still beaming—Ben, Charlie, Tess and Teddy went looking for wedding dresses.

'Because I'm on a roll and I refuse to stop rolling,' Charlie told the bemused Ben. 'An ice cream for you first, and then a wedding dress for our Tessa. I have your Aunty Tess right where I want her and I want everything perfect.'

'Isn't it bad luck for the groom to see the wedding dress before the day? I should go looking for wedding dresses by myself,' Tess said dubiously.

She was outvoted two to one.

'What fun is that?' Charlie demanded. 'We want to

see you dressed like a fairy princess, don't we, Ben? So let's do it.'

It was a ridiculous two hours. Afterwards Tess would remember it as if it had been a dream, a total indulgence in what was, after all, nothing but a fairytale.

In a shop filled with chandeliers and plush white carpet and rows and rows of white lace bridal gowns, she tried on one amazing confection after another, while her boys looked on with admiration.

Ben was just plain dazzled. While some children might have found the whole experience boring, Ben sat solemnly beside Charlie on the gilt chairs provided for advisers, licked his ice cream and did just that. Advised.

'I don't like that bow,' he said, as Tess glided out in a dress that was pure fantasy—all frills and flounces and a vast white bustle adorned with a bow as wide as the dressing room door. 'It makes your bottom look fat.'

'In general I like bottoms,' Charlie said, nodding in grave agreement. 'But I have to agree. Maybe this is taking a good thing a bit far.'

'It looks bouncy,' Ben said. He methodically demolished the last of his ice cream, licked his fingers—a careful child—then walked slowly around his aunt to inspect the said bottom with care. The mechanics of the bustle had him fascinated.

'If you sit down, will you bounce?'

Tess looked behind her and giggled. 'I could try.'

The sales girl sniffed her disapproval, and Tess chuckled again—and went to indulge her menfolk with another.

The next dress had Charlie's eyes popping out with appreciation but Ben disapproved absolutely.

'It doesn't cover enough. Your bumps are going to pop out.'

They were indeed. Tess grinned down at her very exposed cleavage, put a hand up to cover her 'bumps' and escaped to the dressing room before Charlie could say a word.

'Hey, I liked it,' Charlie yelled after her. 'Come back here this minute.'

'Not until I've covered my bumps!'

'Your bumps are great.'

'Pervert!'

'How can I be a pervert when I'm looking at my very own affianced wife?' Charlie complained. 'Ben, is there no justice in the world?'

In the end they chose a dress that all of them loved.

The gown was stunningly simple—deepest ivory silk with a scooped neckline, tiny sleeves and a bodice that curved around Tessa's 'bumps' and down to her waist as if it were moulded to her. Tiny seed pearls accentuated her breastline and, at the back, silk lacing descended from the low scooped neck to soft folds billowing out from her waist. The dress fell in ivory clouds to the floor, sweeping out behind in a luxurious train.

Charlie had discovered it while Tess was trying on her 'bump' dress, and all of them knew on sight that it was Tessa's dress.

But…

'It's pure silk,' Tess faltered, looking anxiously at the sales girl. 'And so rich…' She fingered the gorgeous texture with longing, but there was no way she was game to ask the price. She'd never seen anything so lovely in all her life, but this wasn't for the likes of Tess. It was…

'It's for a society wedding,' she managed. 'Charlie, I can't buy this dress.'

'It's for you.' Charlie rose, striding over to grip Tessa's shoulders under the silk. He turned her and held her so they were both facing the mirror. 'Look, Tessa. This is you.'

'It's not...' Tessa's voice was troubled. The bride in the mirror was someone out of a fairytale. So much had happened so fast. This was a crazy dream...

But Charlie bent his head and kissed the soft curve of her shoulders.

'Yes, it is you, Tess,' he told her, his voice gentling for her ears alone. 'Tess, I never wanted to be Lord Dalston. I swear I didn't. But now I've had the title thrust upon me and the wealth that goes with it, I'm damned if I'll have anyone else for my lady but you. And you're my lady, Tessa Flanagan. In this dress or in nothing at all, you're my lady. I'd love to buy this for you, to wed you in style. Let me do it, because I love you.'

'It looks really pretty,' Ben piped up behind them—and Tess took a last, long look in the mirror—and caved right in.

This was a soap bubble, she thought desperately as she stared into the mirror. It had to burst at any minute, but for now...for now she was being swept along in a flood of emotion so great she could no sooner swim against the flood than she could fly. So...so why not enjoy the sensation?

She spun around in a full circle, her skirts floating outward in a soft, shimmering swirl.

'You really think I look pretty, Ben?' she asked her nephew.

'Yes.' Tessa's nephew was a man of definite views.

Tess took a deep breath, and made her choice.

'Okay, then, my lord. Okay.' Tessa swept Charlie her very deepest curtsey. 'I'll be your lady, my lord. But I still think you're nuts.'

'I'll drink to that,' Charlie said promptly. 'A nutty

lord with a very, very beautiful lady.' He hauled Ben up into his arms and gave him a hug. 'We're doing very nicely here, Ben. We've got ourselves a wife and mother. Now let's see if we can find your Emma and complete our domestic set. One lord, one lady, one lordling and one nanny. How about that?'

After that there were three days. Three blissful days settled back in Borrowdale.

There was still so much to do but now, instead of packing, Tess's activities were redirected. Charlie hauled out Christine's big bed and replaced it with a new one. He repainted the bedroom and insisted on new furnishings.

'Because this will be one of our permanent bases,' he told Tess. 'We have the farm in Australia, the apartment in London, this house, and our castle. Because of Ben, this place has to be where we stay a lot. So let's make ourselves comfortable.'

Tess went along with him because she was too dazed to do anything else. The flood was at full force.

Emma and Ben settled back happily into their rooms upstairs, but their life had changed for the better as well. More and more, Ben ventured down to see what his crazy new aunt and uncle were doing. Charlie had him wielding a paintbrush—in fact, by the Thursday afternoon he had them all paint spattered and happy.

On the Thursday night they ate fish and chips on the living room floor among the packaging from the new furnishings. Ben made a cubby in the packing boxes, then Emma and Ben retired for the night, Charlie made love to Tess in their brand new bedroom and they slept the night through in each other's arms.

But on Friday he left them. 'I have business at the castle,' he told Tess. He kissed her long and hard. 'I'll be away for two days, sweetheart. It's damnable, but if I spend the night at the castle. I can do it in two days, whereas if I keep coming back...'

Tess wriggled in his arms, comfortable as only a woman loved can feel. Crazy or not, she was growing to believe in her soap bubble.

'Will you sleep in the dungeon?'

'No fear.' He grinned. 'I told you, there's a caretaker's residence...'

'With lady caretaker?'

'Uh-oh...' His eyes caressed her. 'Jealous already?' He grinned. 'I told you that, too. Mr and Mrs Humphreys are eighty if they're a day and I did give them notice that I was coming. Mrs Humphreys might just have managed to put sheets on a spare bed by now, though she'll have whinged all the time. You'll meet them soon. You'll love them.'

'Okay.' Tess backed away an inch and fixed her love with a look. 'Just don't you forget me,' she whispered—then she kissed him back, allowing her tongue to wander.

Charlie groaned and had to haul himself away.

'Two days. Not one second more...'

He left, and that afternoon Margot Blainey arrived, to burst the soap bubble.

CHAPTER NINE

IT WAS Ben who saw his grandmother arrive. He was upstairs with Emma, and Tess heard him start to cry. She took the stairs two at a time and found Emma holding the little boy tight in her arms. Emma was as distressed as Ben.

'It's her,' Emma said dully. 'Mrs Blainey. Benny saw her through the window and thinks she's come to take him away.'

'She's not taking you anywhere,' Tessa told Ben, but the little boy wasn't listening. He was clinging to his Em as though life depended on it, and Em was clinging right back. They both saw their fragile happiness disappearing in the face of a dragon.

Well, Charlie wasn't here. It was up to Tess to face their dragon on her own. Tess glanced out the window to make sure they hadn't been mistaken—some hope!—and then went downstairs to face her, summoning up all the dragon-facing fortitude she possessed. Just as well she wasn't wearing pantyhose!

Unfortunately, the dragon was at her imperious best.

Margot Blainey didn't even bother to be polite. She stood on the doorstep and looked at Tess as though she was something the cat had dragged home. 'I don't wish to see you,' she stated flatly. 'I'm here to see your so-called fiancé.'

'Charlie's not here.' Tess squared her shoulders and wished she didn't have paint on her nose. 'So would you like to go away?' she added hopefully.

The woman glared down her long nose.

Tess sighed. This was Ben's grandma. She *did* have a duty to be polite, much as it almost choked her. 'I'm sorry,' she said. 'That was uncalled for. Can I help you?'

'You can give me back my grandson.'

'I can't do that.' Tessa's simmering anger started to build. Good. Anger definitely helped in facing dragons. Especially dragons you were a little bit afraid of.

But, before Tess could stop her, the woman was pushing past into the house. She stopped at the living room door and stared around in horror. Ben's cardboard cubby house, built of packing boxes from their new bedding, took over the Persian rug in the middle of the living room floor. The ornate coffee tables had been pushed aside, and all the fragile ornaments had been removed for safe keeping.

'What have you done to my son's house?' Margot demanded, appalled.

'Mrs Blainey, it's Ben's house now,' Tess told her, her voice gentling. 'I'm sorry if the changes upset you, but that's the way it has to be. Ben's troubled and we're making him happy. That's the only important thing at the moment.'

'You surely don't intend staying here?'

'We might.'

The woman rounded on her. 'Do you realize how much this house is worth as a rental property? It's worth a small fortune. Or rather a large fortune. What I could do with that...'

Her voice died away.

'Maybe.' Tessa's eyes didn't leave her face. 'But if I rent it out, I'll place any rental proceeds in trust for Ben. As I'm sure you'd have directed if you had control of his future.'

The woman's breath hissed out between her teeth, and Tess knew suddenly that Charlie was right when he guessed there was money behind Margot Blainey's bid to control her grandson. With Ben's legal guardian—Tess—safely in Australia, this woman could have taken control and ripped off the estate for all it was worth. This was guesswork. She couldn't be sure.

'I'm sorry,' Tess said again, but her voice was edged with steel as her suspicions firmed.

'No matter,' the woman said flatly, putting a hold on her temper. 'I'll get it back into order as soon as you go back to Australia.'

'I'm not returning to Australia.' Tess braced herself. 'At least, not permanently. Charles and I will stay here most of the time.'

'Well, that's where you're wrong. That's why I wanted to talk to that young man. He's making you fool's promises. If you think Charles Cameron will be bothered with you once he's safely married...'

Silence.

The silence went on and on. Nothing moved.

Upstairs Em was holding Ben in her arms and blocking out the sounds of his grandmother, but even the house seemed to hold its breath.

'What on earth do you mean by that?' Tess asked at last. 'Of all the stupid...'

'It's you who are stupid.'

Good grief. 'I think you'd better leave.' Tess walked to the door and hauled it wide. 'You're being offensive.'

The woman didn't stir. 'I'm not being offensive,' she said, in a voice that was laced with venom. 'I'm being honest. You poor, deluded little fool, do you think someone like Charles Cameron would marry someone like you because he *wants* to?' Her voice rose in incredulity. The idea was plainly ridiculous.

Unconsciously Tess fingered the diamond on her ring finger, and drew strength from its tangible presence.

'Of course he wants to.'

'He wants his inheritance,' Margot said nastily. 'I've done my homework. When you left I put my lawyers onto it. I told them to figure out just how someone like you could get themselves engaged so quickly. And I was right. It's a rush job. Charles Cameron has to be married by the end of next month or he loses his inheritance.'

'I know that.' Tess moistened her suddenly dry lips. 'He told me. There are legal complications about inheriting his castle which don't exist if we marry now. But he doesn't care about the castle. He'd inherit it anyway, eventually, and it's an absolute ruin.'

'Is that all that he told you?' Margot's eyes flared in triumph and Tess suddenly felt sick.

Was that all? Please God, let it be all. She didn't want to hear what the woman had to say next.

'This...this is none of your business. I want you to go.'

'What concerns my grandson is my business, and this concerns my grandson. He'll dump you, girl. He'll marry you and dump you. Take you back to Australia, at a guess, and dump you and my grandson there, and then get on with his high life.'

'He doesn't... It's only a ruined castle...' Tess was way out of her depth. The vague suspicions she'd shoved to the edge of her mind were flooding back in force. Surely Charles couldn't really want her for *her*? It had never made sense. And now this woman was saying there really was a logical reason for his urgency. 'I don't understand.'

'Do you really think he wants to marry?' The woman shoved her hand into her capacious handbag and hauled out a sheath of newspaper clippings. 'These are only a sample of what my lawyer found. Look...' She thrust them into Tessa's hands.

Tess looked and winced.

'You can get *''beautiful''* in hundreds of places,' she'd told Charles when he'd been pressuring her to marry him. 'Someone with your looks and your money...'

She'd been right. It was true. Charles had had *'beautiful'*. These were torn out clippings from society pages, from England, from Australia, from New York. Charles Cameron, heir to the Dalston fortune. Charles Cameron with one beautiful lady on his arm after another.

Margot Blainey watched her flick though the sheath of newspapers and gave a nasty laugh. 'You see? He can get anyone he wants. Only maybe not fast—or maybe he needs someone who's stupid enough to ditch without making a fuss straight afterwards. Someone like you.'

'This isn't...'

But Margot wasn't to be stopped. 'You little fool, he loses a fortune if he doesn't marry. Oh, yes, the castle's entailed and he'll get that anyway. But the land's not. Has he told you about the land?'

'The land...' The nausea and sense of unreality were deepening by the minute.

'There's thousands of acres...' Margot had seen the colour wash from Tessa's face and now she moved in for the kill. 'Mile upon mile of prime grazing land all along the border. All along the fells of Cumbria. And homes. There's a small town near the castle nearly completely owned by the estate. If your precious Lord Dalston is married by the time he turns thirty, then it all goes to him. If not, it's sold to the highest bidder. End of story.'

'I don't...' Tess faltered and stopped. She felt like putting her hands to her ears, anything to stop the dismay flooding through her.

'Do you know how much that land is worth?' Margot Blainey was unrelenting. 'My lawyers did a quick calculation. There's over a hundred smallholdings—tenant farmers. Each on a viable farm. Plus the township. You're looking at millions and millions of pounds. Incredible wealth. Staggering. And he loses the lot if he doesn't marry.'

'I don't believe you. He would have told me.'

'Don't you believe me? Don't you?' The woman snorted. Then she snatched the newspapers out of Tessa's limp hands and threw them at her. They fluttered over the living room floor—over Ben's cubby house. Over Tessa's dreams.

'He'll never support you, girl. Not long term. You'll be dumped just as soon as the wedding's over. Charles Cameron doesn't need a wife. He needs a name on a document. So if you think he intends to care for my grandson...'

'He does.'

'He doesn't. How do you intend to pay for a nanny without him? Or even care for the child? I've done my arithmetic. My lawyer telephoned that ex-flame of yours in Australia. Remarkably enlightening, he was. You're still encumbered with debt. You had to borrow money against your house savings to get here—your fiancé didn't pay for you and the savings are in his name. Do you think he'll let you near them now? According to my lawyer, there's no chance. You're in a mess, and if you think I'm leaving you in charge of my grandson you have another think coming. Give him to me now.'

'No.'

Tess was practically beyond thought but she could think that far. Not that. She might lose Charlie, but she mustn't lose Ben. There was enough strength left within her to know that Ben would be happier poor and with her than he would be with his grandmother.

'No,' she said again. She squared her shoulders. 'I'm

Ben's guardian and I'm a trained nurse. I can always get a job. Ben and I might end up on our own but, even if we do, then that's okay. Ben's parents have left enough for Ben to be properly clothed and educated, and that's all that matters.'

She took a deep breath. 'But whatever we do—whatever our future is—it has nothing to do with you. If you'd like to keep in contact with Ben and I see your approach to him as being loving and concerned, then your contact can continue. I won't keep him from you. But...but for now, I want you to leave this house, and leave us alone.'

'You stupid girl...'

'Just go.'

Margot Blainey had been gone for two minutes before Em and Ben crept into the room. They really were two children, Tess thought, looking at Em's troubled eyes shadowed in her elfin face. They looked like brother and sister, rather than nanny and child, and they were both looking to Tessa.

'We heard,' Em whispered. 'Oh, miss, surely Charlie can't be like that.'

Charlie. Em was halfway to being in love with Charlie herself, Tess thought sadly. She couldn't blame her, any woman would be.

'I don't know...' Tess shook her head as if trying to shake off a bad dream. 'I don't...'

'If it's true, will I have to go?'

The girl held Ben close in her arms, but her white face was tilting upward, as if expecting to be struck. Tess was shaken out of her own misery enough to wonder why.

'You really like this job?'

'Mrs... Christine gave me the job as Ben's nanny

when I was fifteen,' Emma whispered. 'Mr Blainey didn't want me. He said I was too young. But my mum had just remarried and my stepdad didn't want me. He kicked me out. I couldn't get a job, I had no decent clothes and every interviewer thought I looked like a street kid, which I was. I was living under the bridges—in parks. Anywhere. Then one day Christine—Ben's mum—was shopping in Keswick and Ben ran out in front of a car. I grabbed him.' She shrugged. 'Then Christine bought me a meal, and brought me home. I've been here ever since.'

Tess swallowed, and swallowed again. Christine brought me home…

Tess had loved Christine so much, her twin, her other half. Christine had walked away from Australia without a backward glance and teamed up with a family Tessa couldn't stand. Tessa had felt… For the last few years she'd felt as if she'd lost Christine, the Christine she knew. She'd felt the Christine she'd known and loved had been a figment of wishful imagination.

Now, suddenly, she was being handed back the Christine she'd grown up with, the Christine she loved. With this one, tangible gesture of compassion and caring, she could remember her sister with love.

'I want to stay with Ben,' Em whispered. 'Even if you can't pay me. Me and Ben want to be together…'

Oh, help…

Tess stared helplessly at this waif-like child, and she knew, without one glimmer of doubt, that Em had to stay. In a way, Em was just as much a child as Ben was, just as needful of family. And Tess was now responsible for them all.

Shoving her misery aside for the moment, she forced herself to think. Maybe it could work. Maybe…

If what Margot Blainey said was true, then this house

could be rented out for a fortune. Maybe for enough to keep Em as Ben's nanny, at least until he was school-age. Tess would have no compunction spending Ben's money on a nanny.

And that left her where?

Back to nursing. They'd all have to go back to Australia, she decided bleakly, the three of them. She'd go back to her job and Em would take care of Ben while she worked.

It was a future for all of them—of a sort. Better than the streets for Em and his grandmother for Ben.

And for Tess?

What about Charlie?

Misery flooded back. The thought of Charlie left her sick to the core. He'd lied to her. His lawyer had lied.

Damn them both, she thought bleakly. Men couldn't be trusted. Her mother had told her that over and over. Why, oh why hadn't she listened?

Tess tugged the diamond from her left hand and it came free. She shoved it in her jeans pocket and her finger felt naked without it. Dreadful.

'Okay, we stay together,' she said savagely. 'We must. But Em, will you come to Australia?'

'I... Yes.' The girl swallowed. 'Oh, yes. If you want me. But...but what about our Charlie?'

'He isn't our Charlie,' Tess told her, and the anger in her voice was the only thing that kept the tears at bay. 'Charles Cameron lied to me. I'll check what Mrs Blainey told me, but if it's true...if he is trying to con me into marriage just so he can inherit a fortune, then he has nothing more to do with us. If it's okay with you, Em—I think you and me and Ben are a team, a trio, and no one else need apply to join.'

'Will...will you tell... I mean, will you tell *him* that we're going?'

'Oh, I'll tell Charlie,' Tess said bitterly. 'If you take care of Ben, I'll tell him now.'

It took four hours to find Charlie, and by the time she did, Tess was past emotion. All that was left was empty, desolate exhaustion.

He wasn't at the castle. Tess found the caretaker's residence—complete with aged caretakers as Charlie had promised—and was redirected to a farm about two miles down the road.

'Highrigg,' the elderly woman told her. 'It's the outer farm on the north-east boundary.'

'It's one of Ch...one of Lord Dalston's?'

'Oh, glory, yes,' the woman told her. 'They all are, hereabouts. You can drive for half an hour to the north without stepping off Lord Dalston's land.'

He wasn't at Highrigg. A wizened old farmer surrounded by half a dozen farm dogs directed her on. 'His lordship's been here, spreading the good news.' His dour tone told her it was nothing of the sort. 'Gone on to Westfell down the road.'

'He owns this farm?'

'Yeah, more's the pity.' The farmer spat into the dust.

'I don't understand.'

'I've been a tenant farmer all my life,' the farmer told Tess bitterly. 'Paying handsomely into his lordship's rent-roll. Finally I was going to get out of his clutches, but not now.'

'I don't understand.'

'His lordship's found some little tart who's willing to marry him.' The farmer jabbed a boot into the dust and spat again. 'The old lord...see, when he died he directed that the farms be sold on the open market, fair and square like. So I could get me chance to buy the place for meself. Only his new blasted lordship doesn't have to sell up if he marries by the time he's thirty. And now he's found this...this *tart* and he reckons he's the smartest thing since sliced bread. Going round the farms telling us all the great news, and I'll go back to paying rent for the rest of me natural days.'

He spat for the third time, directed her on to Westfell and took himself and his dogs back into the farmhouse, with Tess staring after him in dismay.

She'd come so close to ruining so many lives. So many lives to make one man richer. How dared he!

Anger. Anger was what she needed. Forget the misery. Forget how his body made her feel. Forget anything else but that he'd tricked her. She followed the old man's directions and ended up at the gate of Westfell.

And there he was, standing on the other side of the gate— two hundred yards from the house and obviously just preparing to leave. Charles.

Her love.

Not her love. The man who'd tricked her into believing he loved her, into believing in fairytales.

He looked up as the little car she'd hired approached the gate. He'd driven through already and was about to close it. Now he paused, not recognizing her from a distance but expecting that she'd drive on through, waiting to save her the worry of opening the gate.

He was *so* good looking. Charles stood, leaning on the gate, his black hair whipped by the warm breeze, and his kilt swirling around his legs...

When he saw Tessa at the wheel of her little car, his face broke into the broadest of smiles. A wondrous smile. A smile that might almost be that of a man in love.

Only Tess knew better.

It was a trickster's face and the sooner she got this over with, the better.

Tess climbed from the car and went to tell Charles Cameron, the thirteenth Earl of Dalston, that she wasn't going to save his fortune for anything.

CHAPTER TEN

'HEY, Tess...'

He didn't think anything was wrong. There was joy in his face—and Tess had to steel herself against that joy, tell herself the joy was fake. Armour herself against the sight of him, against the urge to throw herself into his arms and forget everything she'd just been told.

Maybe even a mock marriage was better than no marriage at all.

What was she thinking? For heaven's sake... Tess was an ordinary girl, of ordinary stock, with no money at all. She might have known someone like Charles Cameron wouldn't want her unless there was some good reason, some reason that had nothing to do with loving her. She forced herself to think of all those society photographs Margot Blainey had shown her, and her heart chilled.

'Charles.' She rose from her little car and Charlie knew at once that something was wrong.

'Hell, Tess, what is it?' He took three fast strides toward her but she fended him off with her hands, and backed away. He wasn't to touch her; he mustn't.

'What's wrong?' he said again and Tess shook her head.

'I can't... Charles, I just came to tell you... Margot Blainey came...'

'It's Ben.' He was with her then in two more strides and, regardless of her instinctive recoil, he gripped her shoulders. 'Tess, has she taken Ben?'

'No.'

That got to him, her blank, cold 'no'. He released her

shoulders and stared down at her, and Tessa stared at her toes.

'Then what, sweetheart?'

The tenderness and concern in his voice was nearly her undoing. The last thing she needed was tenderness.

'Charles...' She didn't look up at him; she couldn't. 'Charles, is it true that if I marry you, you stand to inherit over a hundred farms and more houses as well as your castle?'

Charles froze.

'Who told you that?'

'Margot.'

Silence. It was a silence that went on and on, on into the distance, echoing into the distant hills and back to them.

A silence signalling the end.

'It's true, isn't it?' Tess said heavily. 'I've asked. The farmers around here say the same thing. If you're not married by the time you turn thirty, then you can't keep these farms. Can you?'

Charles closed his eyes.

'No, Tessa,' he told her. 'I can't.'

She hadn't wanted to hear that. She'd desperately wanted him to deny it, for somehow Margot Blainey to be wrong.

'You lied to me,' she whispered. 'You lied...'

'I didn't lie, Tess,' he told her. 'It's true about the castle. My uncle left the castle to the National Trust but he can't do it, because of the entailment. I stand to inherit it anyway.'

'But the castle's the least of your problems. Isn't it? You want these farms.'

'Tess...'

'You told me it didn't really matter,' she said heavily. 'That marrying me would make no real difference. It'd just keep a few lawyers at bay.' She stared up at him then, her eyes dark and shadowed in her pale face. 'But it does make a difference, doesn't it, Charlie? You do need to be married.'

'Tess...'

'You do need to be married.' Her voice was heavy with insistence. 'You do want to keep this land.'

He sighed then, a long, weary sigh that went on for ever, and the joy in his face died completely.

'Yes, Tess," he told her. 'I do need to be married. It's important...'

She cut him off. 'You would never have thought of marrying me otherwise?'

There was no way he could lie to her now. Not now. Not with guilt lying all around him, guilt written plainly on his face. 'No, Tess. I wouldn't have thought of it,' he said wearily. 'I've never thought of marrying. It was only this damned stupid clause in the will. But hell...' His hands seized hers and gripped. 'Tess, I swear that was only at the start. I...'

'I don't want to listen.' She broke away from him then and stood, desolate, two feet away, with trouble written all over her face. 'I can't. I'm not listening to you any more. Charlie, I can't trust you...'

That got to him. Like a knife to the heart, that got to him, and he could only agree with her. Hell, he wouldn't trust himself. One last try...

'Tess, you don't understand. I need you to marry me for all sorts of reasons, and the biggest one is that I love you.' He didn't expect her to believe him, though, and she didn't.

'No.' She shook her head. 'Charlie, I'll not be blackmailed into marrying. Or bought.' She shoved her hand into her jeans pocket and brought out the little velvet box. One diamond ring. And handed it back at arm's length. 'This is the end, Charlie Cameron. I might have known love at first sight was ridiculous, something that happens in fairy stories. It doesn't happen in real life. It doesn't happen now. Goodbye, Charlie,' she said bleakly. 'If you need to be married, then you need to find someone else. Not me. I don't want to see you again. Not now. Not ever.'

And she turned and climbed back into her little car—and drove away from her love for ever.

Charlie went back to his castle.

And paced.

Hell!

Hell, hell and hell. What did he do now? Go after her and tell her the truth? Tell her just what was at stake? Hold the loaded pistol at her head instead of just at his? He couldn't. Maybe if he didn't love her so much he could but now...

She'd never believe he loved her for herself. No matter what he told her, she'd never believe it now, and to put such overwhelming pressure on another person was unthinkable.

Especially when that person was Tessa, the woman he loved... Dear God, what was he to do? Silence. There were no answers here. There were no answers at all. It'd have to wait. Somehow he had to put this aching desolation aside. He couldn't follow her. He couldn't!

What was between he and Tessa would have to wait now until this whole sordid mess was over. He'd save what he could, but he wouldn't save it through marriage.

If he sold the farm in Australia...and he sold his US stocks and bonds...his mother's legacy...how much of this could he protect?

He looked out over his lands and Charlie Cameron felt as the first Earl of Dalston must have felt when he put up these staunch stone battlements against invaders all those years ago. It wasn't just the Earl of Dalston he was protecting, but all those around him. Those who depended on him.

The mantle of responsibility was heavy indeed. Too many people depending only on him...

Charlie Cameron put his hand up and raked his fingers wearily though his thick dark hair. He'd never wanted this legacy. Never. And now...now it meant he'd lose his farm in Australia. And worse. It meant...it meant he stood to lose Tessa. It meant that until he turned thirty, he had to leave Tessa Flanagan strictly alone, because blackmail wasn't the thirteenth earl's style.

Three weeks...

Three interminable weeks.

Tess contacted the hospital at Yaldara Bay and arranged for another week's leave. That was all she could manage and so much had to be done. Ben's life and Emma's had to be packed away to be taken to the other side of the world.

'It'd be nice if we could stay here,' Emma said wistfully as she helped Tess pack away Ben's clothing. 'Ben and me like this house.'

Tess sat back on her heels and looked at Emma, trouble written over her face.

'Em, if you don't want to come...I'll write you the best reference so you can get another nanny job here.'

'But I'm still only sixteen and I sound rough,' Em said frankly. 'I'm trying to sound proper and be a good nanny. But I don't sound good yet.'

'You are a good nanny. Ben loves you.'

'Yeah, but...' Emma sighed. 'It's not enough. Not one reference and no qualifications. If I go for another job, I'd never get it. Most nannies now have diplomas and stuff.' She bit her lip. 'No. I'll come with you and Ben. I think I'll like Australia when I get there. It's just...it's such a long way from my mum and everything I know. And I can't see why we can't stay here, in this house. Ben would be happier here.'

'Em, I can't afford to stay in England. Not here.' Over and over, Tess had done her arithmetic and it always came out the same. At home she had a good job with a decent salary. She could rent out this house. With the proceeds she could afford to rent a bigger flat in Yaldara Bay to fit them all, and to pay Emma a decent wage. That way Tess wouldn't be eating into the funds for Ben's education.

But if they stayed here...in this house which all of them loved... With no extravagant rental coming in, there was no way a nurse's salary could cover Emma's wage as well as feed them all, even if Tess could get a job nearby.

There was no choice. They had to go.

'I'm sorry, Em,' she told the girl, 'but there's no way I can...'

But Em was distracted and no longer listening. 'Miss, there's someone coming up the path.'

Tess turned. Whoever had just passed the window was right by the door now and couldn't be seen—but parked outside was a shining black Jaguar.

Charlie's car.

Tess rose to her feet and stared out at the car. A tiny, hopeless prayer started in the far reaches of her heart, and wouldn't be suppressed. Charlie.

But...she didn't want to see Charlie. She mustn't. He was nothing to do with her.

'Will you answer the door, Em?' she asked dully. 'If it's Charlie... If it's Charlie then tell him to go away. I won't see him.'

'Oh, miss, are you sure?'

'I'm sure.'

Em gave her a long, considering stare and then went to open the door. Two minutes later she was back.

'It's not Lord Dalston,' she said and there was disappointment in her voice. 'It's a man who says to tell you his name is Henry from London and he needs to talk to you urgently.'

Henry.

Tess was on her feet in a flash. Henry. Why on earth was Henry here? Had something happened to Charlie? What was Henry doing, coming all the way from London? To see her?

Whatever it was, he wasn't in a hurry to tell her. Henry stood on the front doorstep and twisted his cap in his hands and looked altogether uncomfortable. Em stood behind Tessa and stared over Tessa's shoulder with blatant interest.

'Henry, is something wrong?' It was impossible for Tess to keep the fear from her voice and Henry heard it.

'No, miss. Nothing's wrong. That is...'

'Charlie's okay?'

'Yes, miss. He's fine. He's just made a flying trip to see his uncle's lawyers in London and I've just dropped him off again at the castle.'

'I see.' She didn't see at all. Tess took a deep breath, and decided to make it formal. 'How can I help you, then, Henry?'

'I really need to talk to you, lass,' Henry said desperately. 'Outside.' He cast a despairing look at Em. 'Alone, if you don't mind.'

She shouldn't go with him. She shouldn't. Charlie and the people he employed had nothing to do with her any more. But...

But she must.

'I'll come,' Tess said. Ben was down for his afternoon sleep and the house was quiet. She cast an apologetic look at the bemused Emma, and closed the door behind her.

They walked away from the house, but whatever Henry had to say he wasn't in a hurry to say it. They walked across the road and then onto the little jetty reaching out into Derwent Water. The lake was still and lovely, and a host of little ducks were clustered under the piers. Tess stood at the end of the jetty, the sun on her face, and waited for Henry to say what he had to say.

He said nothing.

There were groups of holidaymakers on the jetty, laughing and feeding the ducks and hopping in and out of the rented rowing boats. Tess stood in the sun and looked at Henry and waited, and Henry looked from the holidaymakers and back to Tess again— almost pleading. Finally Tess took pity on the man.

'How about hiring a row boat? Would you like that?'

That brightened things. Henry considered it an excellent suggestion, and two minutes later they were pulling away from the jetty, Henry wielding the oars like an expert.

Tess leaned back against the cushions in the bow of the boat and watched Henry's troubled face and forced herself to be patient. Whatever was coming, the coming was hard.

'It'll never be any easier, Henry,' she said gently, finally, when they were well away from the jetty. 'So say it.'

Henry looked up at her, his elderly face creased in misery. She smiled encouragingly at him and he sighed.

'Mary was right,' he said softly. 'You are a lass with a difference. A lass with a heart.'

'You and Mary have been talking?'

'Yes.'

'About me? And...' She ventured a guess. 'About my relationship with Lord Dalston?'

'Yes.' There was no hiding his embarrassment. The man was practically puce. 'I told Mary I couldn't do this,' he said desperately. 'But it was either me or Mary had to do it, and she couldn't get away and I was bringing the car up anyway. Mary found out where you were staying. I think she searched his lordship's address book but I had nothing to do with that. It was all Mary's idea.'

'What was all Mary's idea?'

'We want to know...'

This was getting harder by the minute. 'You want to know what?'

'Why you won't marry Mr Charlie,' Henry blurted out. And then he rowed like one possessed. A speedboat would have had trouble keeping up with Henry the way he was rowing.

Tess was silent for a while as they powered on, and then she leaned forward and put her hand on Henry's trousered knee.

'Henry, stop. Ease up. You'll give yourself a hernia.'

'What...?' Henry caught himself. He looked around them. No other boat was in sight. They were practically in the centre of the lake. 'Oh...' He gave a sheepish grin. 'Sorry.' He eased back on the oars.

'I just don't want to be wiped out on the opposite shore.' Tess smiled and hesitated. 'Henry, how do you know that Charlie wants to marry me?'

'He told me.' Henry's colour ebbed and then rushed back. 'Well, in a manner of speaking he told me.' He paused. 'In fact... To be honest, he got himself well and truly drunk.'

'Drunk!' The thought of Charlie drunk was crazy. Totally out of character. But then...maybe she didn't know him as well as she thought she had. After all, he had tried to deceive her.

'You're right, lass.' It seemed Henry could sense her thoughts. 'His lordship doesn't drink to excess. In fact, I haven't seen him under the weather since the night his grandpa introduced him to malt whisky when he was just seventeen. They'd just been to the cricket, you see, and Australia won the ashes. They were the merriest pair of drunks you've ever seen in your life. But this time...'

'This time he wasn't merry?'

'No, miss, he wasn't,' Henry said bluntly. 'I put him to bed and he told me everything.' He sighed. 'Some of it I knew, of course. But not all. And not how he felt about you. Well, I told Mary and Mary said maybe he hadn't been honest with you, and she thought that maybe if you knew...'

'Knew what?'

Henry closed his eyes, and opened them again. 'Well, maybe you know what I'm going to say already. But...do you know the terms of the late lord's will?'

Tessa's smile faded. 'I think I do. The will leaves everything to Charlie—but only if he marries by his thirtieth birthday.'

'That's right.' Henry looked sightlessly out across the water, refusing to look at her. 'Lass, to understand that, you have to understand the late Lord Dalston. He was...well, to put it bluntly, the man was a killjoy. He got pleasure out of making others miserable. He didn't get on with his father or his brother or his nephew, and he saw Mr Charlie as a playboy. I doubt Mr Charlie's ever been what you'd call a playboy, but he's enjoyed life and been in the society pages enough to give his uncle that impression. Hence the marriage clause.'

'I already know this.'

'Yes. But do you know just how much depends on Mr Charlie marrying? *Exactly* how much?'

Tessa grimaced. Here it was again. Financial blackmail.

'I can't let that alter my decision,' she said stiffly. 'No matter how much is involved, I won't be bought. I imagine Charles will have enough to survive on without me marrying him.'

Henry stared. 'Well, yes. He'll have enough and to spare. If he wasn't a self-sacrificing fool, that is. But that's hardly the issue. It's not Mr Charlie's future at stake here.'

'Not...' Tessa stared. 'Not Charlie's...'

'It's his damned sense of honour.' Henry groaned. 'He won't let you be pressured. But Mary and I... We thought if you love him anyway... Well, you should know the facts.'

Tess stared, bemused. 'And the facts are?'

'The facts...' Henry took a deep breath. 'Well, in total, the estate consists of the castle and the land and the extra property. A hundred or so small farms and more houses. Tenanted, they are. The old lord was tight-fisted—didn't put anything into them at all—but they still bring in a tidy bankroll. The old lord left them to Mr Charlie, and the castle too, as long as he's married.'

'And if he's not?'

'Then everything's to be sold and the money used to restore the castle exactly as it was when it was first built. And then the castle's left to the National Trust.'

'Good grief.' Tessa sat back and stared. 'Good grief!'

'Only the castle can't be left away from Mr Charlie,' Henry said miserably. 'It's entailed. Old Lord Dalston was indulging in wishful thinking when he put that bit in. About the castle going to the National Trust. So if he's not married, then Mr Charlie still ends up with the castle.'

'And that won't bring him much,' Tessa said grimly. 'I can see...'

'No, but you can't.' Henry leaned forward, desperate to make her understand. 'You can't. If he doesn't marry, then he stands to gain. Mr Charlie will be sole owner of a wonderfully restored castle—a tourist attraction that folk would come from all over the world to see. It'll bring him a fortune. He'll have no bad press about selling the farms—after all, it wasn't him who put them on the market. And he'll be an incredibly rich man.'

Tess frowned. 'But...then I don't...I don't understand.'

'Because the castle's his anyway, the will makes him rich. But he doesn't want it.' Henry paused. 'You see,' he said slowly, 'even though the will is null and void when it comes to the castle, the rest of it still stands. Mr Charlie's had legal advice and he can't get out of it. If he doesn't marry, then the farms must be sold and the proceeds used for castle restoration. Every farm. Every piece of freehold property the old lord possessed. And with the price of land and the old houses in the National Trust villages around here, they'll go for a fortune.'

'But...' Tess bit her lip. 'I've met some of the farmers. Or at least one. Some of them want to buy their farms.'

Henry snorted. 'They might want to, but can they? Unlike his late lordship, Mr Charlie would agree at once to them buying their own farms, and given his choice he'd see they had generous terms and time to pay. He doesn't see himself as a feudal overlord.'

'So why can't he...?'

'The stipulation in the will is that everything's sold at

current market price. Many of these farmers have no idea what these places'll fetch at auction. There's an overseas group interested in setting up a fishing and grouse-shooting resort... Putting all the farmers off their land. They'll pay what it takes. And it's making Mr Charlie miserable. He loves this land and his grandfather taught him to treat his tenants as his family. He's breaking his heart over it. And worse.'

'Worse?'

'He'll try to save them. He intends to sell everything he owns to buy the farms back,' Henry said grimly. 'He's working himself to the bone trying to figure out ways and means of keeping the farmers on their land. He's been home to Australia and back again, seeing bank mangers both here and there. He'll mortgage himself to the hilt to try and keep as many farmers on the land their families have farmed for generations.'

'Can he do that?' Tess asked, horrified.

'In part. He intends to try. And maybe he'll save fifty or sixty farms. But then the money going into the castle restoration will be *his* money and he'll be in debt for life. And still there'll be scores of families left who'll lose their land. He can't buy them all at market prices. It's just not possible.'

Tess stared, appalled.

'Scores...'

'At least forty,' Henry repeated miserably. 'Me and Mary included. The London house will go and he'll never be able to buy that back. He could buy four farms with the proceeds from the London house. The farm in Australia goes, too. He's instructed his agent to sell everything.'

Tessa's breath caught in her throat. All this...*all this* responsibility had been resting on Charlie's broad shoulders, while she'd thought him rich and carefree and...

And a liar!

He hadn't lied at all. She thought back over what Charlie and his lawyer had told her and realized with horror that they hadn't lied at all!

'I... And I could stop this?'

'Only if you'll marry him by the time he's thirty,' Henry told her. 'But there's only one week to go. I know it's a huge thing, but Mary said you were halfway to being in love with him and she's guessing he's in love with you. Well, we both know he is. He said your name over and over when he was drunk. Said he's not going to pressure you—that it wouldn't be right.'

'But...'

Henry wouldn't be interrupted. 'Mary says it's as plain as the nose on your face that you're meant for each other.' Henry met her look with eyes that were honest and direct, not a hint of pretence. 'But Mr Charlie says he won't be blackmailing you into any marriage. Which I'm not,' Henry added morosely as if he held out no hope at all for a happy ending. 'I'm just telling you the facts. It's up to you to decide what to do with them.'

What to do...

They didn't speak again while Henry slowly rowed her back to shore.

What hope? thought Henry, as he watched her face. What hope? He'd told Mary that he thought it was a wild goose chase—to come all this way to plead on Charlie's behalf. But then, it wasn't only Charlie's future he was fighting for here, it was the future of a hundred families. It was his future and Mary's future. He watched Tessa's face and a glimmer of hope stirred in the far recesses of his mind. He mustn't let himself hope. He mustn't.

But then he was pulling up at the jetty and Tessa was leaning forward again, her face alive and urgent.

'Henry, where's Charlie now? Is he still at the castle?'

'He's going through the books at the caretaker's residence,' Henry told her. 'Looking at who owns what, trying to figure out just how many of his tenants can afford to buy their own land. If there's any who can,' he added morosely. 'Which I doubt.'

'You wouldn't be going back there?'

Henry's head jerked up. His eyes came alive.

'I would, lass. I certainly would.'

'Take me with you,' Tessa said softly. 'Let's just see what we can do.'

CHAPTER ELEVEN

CHARLIE...

Tessa sat in the rear of the big Jaguar and hugged her knees all the way to the castle. She hadn't changed her clothes. She was still wearing the paint-spattered jeans Henry had found her in. She'd told Em where she was going and asked her to take care of Ben while she was away—and watched joy wash over the girl's face.

'Oh, miss, of course we'll be all right by ourselves. Mr and Mrs Blainey left me all the time with Master Ben.'

'I'll be back tonight.'

'No.' Em hauled herself up to her full five foot two inches and glared. 'No. You stay until you've got that diamond back on your finger, miss. He's too good. I knew he couldn't be doing you down. Oh, miss, Mr Charlie's *that* cute, and in that kilt...' She blushed bright pink and hugged Ben to her. 'Fight for him, miss,' she said fiercely. 'He's worth it.'

He was, Tess thought miserably. He is. He could have *made* her marry him. She knew he could... If he'd told her what was at stake—all those farms—all those lives—then of course she would have married him.

But that wouldn't have suited him. Holding a gun to her head...holding the fate of all those families.

She had made a phone call before she left Borrowdale. The call had been to Edwin Roberts, Charlie's lawyer in Penrith.

'Mr Roberts, the forms that Charles and I signed two

weeks ago,' she had said diffidently. 'The forms for getting married?'

'Yes, miss?' And Tessa had heard the lawyer holding his breath on the end of the phone.

'Did you cancel them? I mean, if we were still wanting to be married before Charlie's birthday...'

The lawyer's breath had been released in one long sigh. 'No, my dear, I haven't cancelled a thing. His lordship instructed me to, but I thought... I hoped... They don't need to be cancelled until the last minute. If there's any chance at all...'

'There's a chance,' Tess had said grimly. 'Don't cancel. No matter what his lordship says.'

'Oh, my goodness...' Amazingly, Tess had heard a thread of laughter in the lawyer's dry and gravelly voice, and a very real pleasure. 'My dear, I believe, in this instance, it would give me considerable happiness to disobey his lordship. And may I wish you the very best of luck?' Then the lawyer's smile had died out of his voice. 'You may well need it,' he had added. 'His lordship's stubborn and exhausted and not thinking straight.'

'Do you mean...?' Tess had thought this through. 'Do you mean he doesn't want to get married? Really?'

'I believe he does wish to be married. But not for the inheritance. I think that's just the trouble,' the lawyer had told her gravely. 'I believe for the first time in his life, his lordship finds the thought of matrimony attractive and the thought of you being forced into anything against your will is abhorrent. And, as I said, I believe he's too exhausted to think rationally any more. So, as I said, my dear, good luck.'

That had been an hour ago. Now they were approaching the castle and Tessa was becoming more and more tense by the minute. Surely she wouldn't need good luck. Tess hugged her knees tighter as the road twisted into the hills before them and she tried to think of what she'd say.

Stupid, chivalrous fool.

Beloved twit!

But how could she make him see sense?

Charlie was in the back office of the caretaker's residence. The elderly woman met both Tess and Henry at the door and offered to fetch him.

'No, Edith,' Henry said heavily, watching Tessa's strained face. 'Take Miss Tessa through and don't announce her. Just show her where to go.'

'But...'

'Just do it, Edith,' Henry ordered. He met the caretaker's eyes and sent her a silent, urgent message. 'Just do it.'

So Edith showed Tess through the big, rambling house—out to the back to a huge shelf- and book-lined room that obviously held the estate records. The housekeeper opened the door, cast Tessa one long, curious look and disappeared.

And Tess was left with her love.

Charlie.

'Charlie...'

He hadn't heard her come. Now, as she said his name, he swivelled on his chair and stared.

'Tessa...' He half rose, and the look in his eyes said it all, said all Tessa would ever want to know.

But then the look died, and he sank back onto the chair.

'Tessa,' he repeated, and the joy was gone. His voice was flat and infinitely weary. 'What are you doing here?'

Tess took a deep breath. The lawyer had said Charlie was exhausted. He had been right; her love looked downright haggard. And there was no easy way to do this.

'I've come to ask if I can have my diamond back,' she said softly. 'I was a fool to return it. I'd like to wear it again.'

Silence. And still the look in Charlie's eyes was blank.

He was exhausted beyond belief, Tess thought, watching him closely. Exhausted past rational thought. There were dark shadows on his face and the skin across his broad cheekbones was stretched tight. His hair was tousled and unkempt—as if he'd been raking his fingers through and through in despair—and his kilt and open necked shirt looked as if they'd been slept in. She looked down at the mounds of paperwork on his desk and knew that he hadn't been gaining any pleasure from his bookwork at all.

Now he was so caught up in his misery that he hardly saw her.

'You don't want to marry me,' he said flatly.

'I do.' She took a step toward him but he shook his head and held up his hands—as if fending her off.

'Tess, I tried to trick you.'

'Charlie...'

'No!'

Damn him, why didn't he move? He sat there like stone and there was an aura about him that refused to allow Tess closer. She longed to walk over to him and take that weary face between her hands—to kiss away the exhaustion and the worry. But the invisible armour was all around him.

'Charlie, I know,' she said gently. 'I know what you tried to do. You tried to make me believe the castle was all that's at stake. But I know what's really at stake. I know why you need to be married and I can't believe I was such a fool to doubt your integrity. It's not your fortune. It's your people's livelihoods. Henry told me everything.'

'Henry...' Still that look of blank rejection.

'Henry came to see me. He told me all about the will. He told me just what happens if you don't marry.' Tess took a deep breath. 'Charlie, marry me,' she said softly. 'There's no need to make these sacrifices. Marry me.'

'You don't want to...'

'I want to marry you more than life itself,' Tess said gently. 'I have since the first time I saw you. Then, when I thought...when I thought you were marrying me for money it seemed so hard... Even though I thought you must be a rat, it was almost impossible to walk away, to hand back your diamond. But now... Charlie, if you'd said...'

'If I'd told you the truth, then you'd have married me?'

Tess tilted her chin. 'Of course. I'll marry you now.'

'Why?'

Good grief! What was wrong with him? Was he so exhausted—so stressed—that he couldn't see? Couldn't see how much she wanted him? He sat with that blank look of misery on his face and she couldn't get past it.

'I want to marry you because I love you. And because...'

'Yes, and because...' He finally moved then, rising and striding over to face her. He placed his hands on her shoulders but he didn't pull her close. The look in his eyes was of anger, and of despair. 'Because Henry's been to see you and told you what's at stake. Because the farmers will lose their land. Because it's the *kind* thing to do.'

'Because of all of those reasons,' Tess said flatly. 'But mostly because I love you.'

He was hardly listening. Despair was driving him to a point where reason didn't work. 'So how can I believe that?' he flung at her. 'How can you believe me when I say I love you? Tess, this is damnable. If we marry like this, it'll hang over us for the rest of our lives and I won't let it. My uncle is not going to sour our marriage like he soured all of his own life. I might have known he'd get to me like this.' Charlie's grip tightened and he looked down into her eyes, then he sighed.

'Tessa, this is impossible,' he said gently. 'I've thought about it. God knows, I've looked at it from every angle possible. But it won't work. If this threat wasn't hanging over my head, then I wouldn't have thought of marriage, and there's the honest truth.' He sighed. 'And I don't...I don't know. I honestly don't know...'

'You don't know if you want to marry me?'

'I don't know anything any more,' he burst out. 'Since I last saw you I've been back to Australia. I've been round each and every one of my farms. I've spent days and days with accountants and financial advisers. I can't see straight any more, Tess.' He closed his eyes and his hold on her shoulders loosened. He gripped her hands, and she felt a shudder raft thought his whole body.

'The truth is, Tess, I can't see straight, but I know enough to figure it's unfair to embroil you in this mess. If, after my birthday—after the dust settles on this whole disaster—then maybe...' Once again, that shudder. 'Maybe we can sort something out. But hell, Tess, it'll be... You'll have Ben. You'll be back in Australia...'

'You'll come to Australia?'

'I'm selling the farm in Australia. There won't be any spare cash. Maybe you'd be better off with your careful Donald after all.'

'Charlie, don't be crazy!' Tessa's voice was urgent. She was fighting his exhaustion. Fighting his crazy sense of nobility. 'You have to marry me. You must!'

'I told you, Tess...I'm not embroiling anyone else in this mess. Not now. Now ever. Now....go. Please?'

The look in his eyes was beyond pain, and there was nothing for Tessa to do but to turn around and leave.

Henry met her outside the study door, and one look at her face was enough to tell him that his plan hadn't worked.

'Henry, he won't...' Tessa's voice broke on a sob. 'Oh, the fool...I can't make him see...'

'That you love him?'

'That I love him,' Tess said forlornly. 'He's forgotten. He's forgotten what we have. He can't see anything but this damned threat...'

'You can't blame him,' Henry told her. 'If you knew what it's been like... As each of the farmers has learned of the conditions of the will they've been making personal pleas. Save-my-land pleas. Word's out on what this foreign consortium's prepared to pay, and the farmers know they can't compete. Family after family have been here begging, and he's known them all his life and there's only so many farms he can save. He hasn't slept. He's past seeing anything but disaster. I hoped...'

'I don't see how I can't get past it,' Tess said bleakly. 'So little time...'

Henry sighed, and tried a weak attempt at a smile. 'Well, miss, you tried and I can only thank you. I guess... Well, it's our trouble now, not yours. Would you like me to take you home?'

'Will he stay in there?' Tess asked. 'Does he come out for dinner? Does he stop?'

'Only to go out to the farms,' Henry told her. 'At sunset he goes up to the castle, every night. He walks up to the castle and stands on the battlements and stares out over his inheritance. Every night he comes back looking more and more like death. Edith was afraid... For a couple of nights there Edith swore he'd jump, but our Mr Charlie is made of sterner stuff than that. I told her there was no fear...'

'Oh, if only...' Tess shook her head. 'There must be some way I can jolt him out of this and make him see reason. Some way...'

Then she stopped dead.

Edith swore he'd jump...

'Henry,' she said in a voice that wasn't quite her own. 'Did you say Charlie went up to the castle every night at dusk?'

'Yes, miss, just as the sun sets. He's not eating a lot, miss, but Edith takes him supper about nine. He walks up to the castle, and then comes back and works until he falls asleep through sheer exhaustion. He doesn't go to bed. Just sleeps at his desk.'

'You think he'll go to the castle tonight?'

'I'd guess so...'

'Then I'm not going home,' Tessa said flatly, a crazy plan forming in the back of her mind and growing. Growing crazier by the minute. 'If you and Edith can put up with me, then I'm staying right here, and I'll need your help.'

Dusk.

Charlie nearly didn't go to the castle.

It was torture, he told himself, as he pushed away his uneaten supper. Torture to walk up to the castle and look out over the farms that he was responsible for, the farms that would soon be lost for ever. It was torture to take the time to think of Tessa.

Why had she come? Henry had no right to have told her what was hanging over them all.

His time with Tessa was like some sweet, far-off dream now. She'd become an unreality in the middle of all this too-real mess that clamoured for his attention, a dream he couldn't afford to distract himself with.

He wouldn't go to the castle. Hell, there was so much work to do here...

But the sun was sinking, the room was claustrophobic and the figures in the books were dancing before his eyes. There was only so much a man could do. He'd take an hour off, he told himself. An hour out of the nightmare and then come back here for the rest of the night.

He left the house and walked slowly up the winding road to the castle. The castle looked lovely in the soft evening light, the ruins grey and ghostly against the sunset.

Charles had a sudden vision of how it would be—restored to mediaeval splendour, surrounded by car parks and tourist shops and tourists...

It should be retained *'as is'*, he thought desperately. Retaining in an unrestored state was a new philosophy of heritage preservation but here it appealed enormously. Maintain the castle exactly as is, allowing no more decay. There was no way this castle could ever be rebuilt as it had been in days gone by. Too much had disappeared and records were sparse. So why pretend? Restored, it would be nothing more than a new castle built about some ruins. A sham of a tourist attraction.

Charlie knew that when it was 'restored' he wouldn't want to come here. The ghosts from long ago would disappear in disgust, leaving it to tourists.

Still, for tonight it was as he loved it, as it had been since his childhood and as his grandfather had first shown it to him. His grandfather was one of the ghosts, Charlie thought sadly, knowing how distraught the old man would have been if he'd been able to see into the future.

Charlie climbed slowly up to the battlements and stood silent, letting the last rays of the sun shine on his face and feeling exhaustion and hopelessness sink over him like a mantle. Hopeless. He shouldn't have come.

The silence went on and on. The ghosts weren't around tonight. Maybe they'd left already, in fear of what was to come.

'You and me both, ghosts,' Charlie whispered to the silence. 'I'm sorry, guys. I can't help this. I can't help *you.*'

So Charles Cameron, thirteenth Earl of Dalston, turned and walked down from his castle. This was the last time he'd come, he told himself, he wouldn't come again.

He was two hundred yards down the road from the castle when he heard the call.

At first Charlie thought he was dreaming. He'd walked out between the vast stone pillars where once troops had marched off to battle and returned. Once it had been a splendid road, now it was merely a track hewn between the pillars, and the crumbling ruins on either side were covered with the white rose of York. It was a place of peace. The troops had long gone. Charlie expected only silence.

But there it was again. Unmistakeable. A faint, woman's cry drifting from above.

'My lord, don't leave me.'

How she'd had the courage, Tessa could never, now or afterwards, figure out. How she'd found the strength to lie in seclusion, hidden by the brambles, while her love stood silent and morose on the wall. Then, as he'd left, she'd scrambled up high on the battlements. High. Higher than she'd ever been before, and with fumbling fingers had done what she had to do. Then she'd called.

Charlie heard. Far below, he turned slowly and looked

up, and Tessa was there, high on the battlement—dear God, she was so near the edge...

There wasn't a stitch of clothing on her lovely body.

Charlie stared upward. Tess seemed totally unconcerned with her nakedness. All she saw was her love, and he was leaving. Her voice called out over the ruins, echoing out into the valley below.

'My lord, don't leave me. My lord...I can't live if you leave me.'

'Tessa...' Charlie stared up, appalled. 'Tessa...'

Where she was standing wasn't safe, Charlie thought desperately. He'd seen the loose stones up there...

No!

But Tessa took another step toward the crumbling edge.

'My lord, don't leave me.' Over and over she called, as Eleanor had called all those centuries before. 'I can't live if you leave me. Come back to me.'

She held out her arms in ancient entreaty, a lady entreating her lord to stay. Her love... Another step...

'Tess, don't move. *Don't move!*' Dear God, those stones were crumbling. Didn't she know those stones were crumbling? 'Tessa, go back...'

Tessa didn't hear. 'My lord...,' she called in an eerie echo. 'Come back...'

'No!' Charles had been up there not ten minutes before. Those stones *could fall*... Any minute now they'd give.

'Don't move!' He was flying—his long legs pounding up the track and his kilt flying. 'Tessa, *don't move*!' But the last thing he saw as he hurled through the castle entrance and disappeared into the thickets that masked the tower staircase was his love taking one more step out to her doom.

She didn't fall.

Charles burst out from the tower like a ball from a cannon. And stopped dead. There she was. His lovely—gloriously lovely—gloriously alive Tessa Flanagan, only now she wasn't looking out to the track below. She was turned and waiting, her eyes eager and her arms outstretched.

'My lord,' she whispered as he burst out on to the battlements and stopped dead. It was too much. Her lips gave the faintest twitch into the dimples in her blushing cheeks. She felt... Well, it was impossible to feel not a little ridiculous. 'My love, I thought you'd never come.'

Charlie gaped. There was nothing else for it. His breath was coming in harsh, jagged gasps. He'd never run nor climbed so fast. He'd moved with superhuman speed. And here was his lovely Tessa, stark naked, and with wanton invitation in her eyes. And...surely...*a trace of laughter*? She was still standing on the crumbling edge. Still... But...

'You're standing on a plank,' he managed, staring down at her naked feet. A solid wooden plank was stretched out from the safety of the solid stone walls to the crumbling edge where she'd stood and called her wild entreaty. She'd been on a solid plank. In no danger at all...

'I may be in love,' Tessa said with quiet dignity, and the twitch around her lips twitched again, all by itself, 'but I'm not crazy. I might be of use to you as a bride, my lord, but I can't see you've any use at all for a corpse three storeys down.' She allowed herself to smile then, that daft, lovely bewitching smile that had his heart doing somersaults, and she held out her arms for him once again.

'So are you going to take me, my lord?'

'Tessa...'

'This is a discount offer,' she said. 'You know. Ten

per cent off. Well, I'm ten per cent off. In case you haven't noticed, all my clothes are gone.'

'Where are they?' he asked, fascinated almost to speechlessness, and Tess chuckled and pointed to the edge.

'Somewhere down there. I don't need 'em. Are you going to marry me?'

'I don't...'

'Charles, take me now or something dire will happen,' she warned. She gave a mock frown. 'I'm not very warm. I think there's something wrong with the central heating up here on these battlements. Are you sure our lovely Eleanor didn't die of goosebumps rather than tumbling down to her doom?'

'Tessa...'

She put her hands on her naked hips and glared. Then she made herself smile, made herself keep it light, when she was fighting for the most important thing she'd ever fought for in her life. 'Charles, do you want me or not?' she said pragmatically. 'I'll have you know I've gone to a lot of trouble to set this up. Henry and I had to haul this ruddy great plank up here and hide it at the other end of the wall so you wouldn't see it. Then I had to lug it into place by myself after you'd gone down. It took so much time that I thought you'd be back to the house before I could get my clothes off—and then I'd be calling after the moon.'

'Tessa...'

'If you won't marry me then I'll make this a habit,' she said severely. 'I've decided. I'll be up here naked every night until you agree. I could get to be a tourist attraction, all on my own.'

'Tessa...' Charlie was a man right out of his depth. He shook his head, bewildered. He was so exhausted he wasn't sure he was even seeing straight.

'You keep saying that,' she complained. 'But you never do anything.'

'What...?' Charlie's voice was strangled. 'What do you want me to do?'

'You could try kissing me,' Tessa said hopefully. 'That'd be a good start. And it might warm me up a bit.' Then she sighed. 'Charles Cameron, will you stop staring at me like I'm some ghost. I'm not a ghost. I'm Tessa Flanagan, the girl you picked up on a plane and asked to marry you, and who agreed and who slept with you without even a contraceptive because she's so besotted with you that her toes curl. She'd think it was an honour to carry your child.'

Tess took a deep breath, her eyes never leaving her love's, and she smiled. 'Charlie, she couldn't think of anything better in life than being your wife. And she couldn't give a toss whether you have a castle or a hundred castles, or even no castle at all, but she's marrying you anyway and you'd better just shut up and get on with it, Charles Cameron. Hug me or I'll die right on the spot from goosebumps and my ghost will haunt you for ever.'

She launched herself right into his arms, and her heart missed three beats. But they were three beats that need never have been missed. Because Charlie was laughing and the exhaustion and shock were falling away as all nightmares eventually do. He was locking her naked body to him in a hug that enveloped every inch of her, and joy was washing over his face like a blazing light.

He was kissing her and she was kissing him back, reaching up on her tiptoes to deepen the kiss—to claim Charlie Cameron as her own. And he was her own. Her arms held him tight, he was her man and Tessa had just taken the craziest risk in the world, but it was working and there was no going back.

This was where she wanted to be for the rest of her life.

'Charlie...'

'Mmm.'

It was some time later, some considerable time later, when speech was possible between them again.

Only just possible, but possible.

'Will you marry me?'

'Hey, I'm supposed to do the asking,' Charlie told her, hugging her lovely body closer.

'You already did. Now it's my turn. I said yes. Now it's your turn to say yes. Say yes, Charlie.'

'Yes, Charlie.'

'Dope.' She hugged him hard. 'But you still said yes. It'll do. I heard it, among all your ancestors too. There's no getting out of this. I can just hear all those ancient Earls of Dalston lining up to nod their approval.

'Of their heir kissing naked ladies on the battlements?'

'They're jealous as hell. I'll bet we have some very jealous ghosts here.' Then Tessa's nose wrinkled as a thought struck. 'Charlie, if I'm not mistaken, you can see these battlements from the house. Am I right?'

'You can see up here from about five miles away.' Charlie hugged his bride hard against his chest, cradled her nakedness against him.

'You mean...'

'I mean I think our engagement's public.' Charlie swept her right up into his arms then, and cradled her against his chest. He stood, bare legs splayed beneath his kilt, holding his naked lady high for all to see.

'I guess this is a public announcement,' he told her lovingly. 'I hereby present my bride to the world.'

'Well...' Tess was finding it difficult to breath. 'It

beats a notice in *The Times*,' she managed. 'Can we get married up here?'

'I thought we were getting married in Australia.'

'Let's do both,' Tessa chuckled and slithered her hand underneath her lover's shirt, and started to undo buttons. 'Lets have heaps of weddings, starting with one now.'

'What, now...?' Charlie stared. Her fingers were under his shirt, sending unmistakeable messages. Then they fell to the buckle of his kilt. His body was heating up like a furnace, but... 'Tess, these stones are damned hard and there are brambles...'

'Not in the dungeon.' She chuckled and her fingers kept right on moving.

'The dungeon's cold.'

'There's a mattress down there and a pile of bedclothes a mile high. And it's really dark.' She reached up and kissed him. 'One candle. That's all we're allowed.'

'One...'

'I had Henry bring everything over earlier,' she said demurely. 'Just in case.'

Charles stared down at her, speechless. 'I don't believe this. I'm being seduced.'

'You'd better believe it, Charlie Cameron, and you'd better get used to it. Once a day or more, for the rest of our lives, I'll seduce you every night until you're ninety, and every morning you can seduce me right back.'

'You're kidding.'

'Would I kid about something so serious?' Tess linked her arms around her lover's neck and held. 'Charlie, take me to your dungeon. I need to be your prisoner. Badly.'

'My prisoner...my Tess...' Finally he smiled, the last of the exhaustion slipping right away as if it had never been. Charlie gave a long, low whoop of triumph, kissed her deeply and then he strode down the steps two at a time, his lady in his arms.

'Well, what are we waiting for?' he laughed as his long legs made mincemeat of the stairs. 'Tessa Flanagan, you are going to make *some* lady for my castle.'

'All I need is to make your bride by Friday,' she whispered.

'Bride by Friday...' Charlie stopped dead, halfway down the stairs, and stared. Then his eyes darkened with passion and he bent to kiss her so deeply that he took her breath right away.

'Tessa Flanagan, you might be my bride by Friday, but you're also going to be a bride for the rest of your life,' he said, his passion lacing his voice with the solemnity of a vow. '*My* bride for the rest of your life. Starting now.'

The lone piper stood high on the north tower, bagpipes ready, as Charles Cameron, the thirteenth Earl of Dalston, stood on the battlements of his castle, waiting for his lady.

This was their formal wedding. Their second.

'We'll marry before my birthday,' Charlie had announced. 'One wedding to keep the lawyers happy, and then we'll marry again afterwards, properly, with no pressure at all. So no man can ever say I married you under duress or you married me under duress, my lovely Tessa.'

So they'd flown to Australia and married before Charlie's birthday in an informal celebration on the beach. The embryonic family—Em and Ben and Tess and Charlie—had enjoyed a crazy, wonderful, foursome honeymoon on the northern beaches until Tess was sure the last traces of exhaustion had faded from her husband's face.

Then they'd returned to England, relaxed, sunburned and happy, to 'do it in style'.

And style there was. Charlie asked Henry and Mary to organize 'a proper lordly wedding' while they were away, and Mary and Henry did them proud.

The whole of Cumbria and Yorkshire and the south of Scotland seemed to have been invited. Every tenant farmer. Every neighbour. Every friend they'd ever had. They were gathered now into the newly cleared castle forecourt, waiting for the bride.

They were watching Charlie waiting for his bride.

Every face was looking upward, watching this handsome young man in full Scottish regalia—Charles Cameron, thirteenth Earl of Dalston—the new lord of this castle.

There wasn't one of them who didn't feel a quiet sense of satisfaction that this was right. This was the new order and it was how things should be, a new lord waiting for his lady in his castle, with his people.

All of his people would watch this wedding. Emma and Ben. Mary and Henry. The elderly lawyer from Penrith, beaming in satisfaction at losing all that business. Even Mrs Blainey had graciously decided to adorn the event with her presence. They'd sent her an invitation because, after all, she was Ben's grandmother and she couldn't hurt him now.

But Charles had no eyes for those below. He watched the approach to the castle.

Then she came. As the car appeared in the distance, the first full notes from the bagpipe echoed out over the valley—as bagpipes had sounded across this valley for generations. The sound from the pipes was full of lives past and the promise of life to come.

The Jaguar pulled to a halt at the castle entrance. Henry bustled around to usher Tessa forth—Tessa in her wonderful dress chosen that magic day such a short, sweet while ago.

Tess was followed by Em as her bridesmaid, blushing and deliriously happy, with Ben as pageboy clutching Em's hand. With *his* Em and *his* Tess—and *his* Charlie playing dress-ups on the castle walls—Ben was game for anything.

This was his new family and Ben thought it was just fine.

Then Henry, his face proud fit to burst, was leading his lady forth, into the castle, up the tower stairs.

Forth to where the piper stood, and the vicar stood.

And where the new lord of this castle was waiting to claim his lady.

Copyright © Harlequin Enterprises Limited 1997
All rights reserved